CHRISTMAS ANGEL JOY

Morris Fenris

Christmas Angel Joy
Three Christmas Angels Book One

Copyright 2019 Morris Fenris, Changing Culture Publications

Table of Contents

Prologue

Guardian Angel School

Heaven

"Hallelujah! Amen!"

The sound of the voices faded away as everyone paused, serene smiles upon their faces.

"Very nice. Let's all take a few moments to ourselves before the celebration starts. Polish your halos. Fluff your wings. Practice your smiles." The choirmaster smiled at them before leaving the room.

Matthias watched as the angels that were part of the angelic chorus departed the choir room, and then he frowned as three little white robed angels snuck out the side door. He was debating about following them when a voice spoke from behind him.

"I wouldn't waste any time going after them. Those three look like they're up to something. I thought this was supposed to be a celebration and yet, they look as if they are preparing for a funeral mass."

Matthias turned and nodded his head, "I was just thinking that same thing. I was hoping to have a quiet Christmas season, but with those three…"

"…there is no such thing as *quiet*."

Matthias nodded and then sighed before heading for the same door where the trio had made their escape. Alexander, the angel in charge of the guard, chuckled and then headed for the courtyard and his post for the rest of the day's celebration. Rather than celebrating Christmas on December 25th only, Heaven celebrated for the entire month. Matthias looked forward to partaking in today's celebration,

5

but first, he had three wayward angels to round up.

He watched the last of the trio slip around the hedge at the back of the school. Pausing beside a fountain on the other side of the courtyard, he kept his distance for the moment but made sure he had a clear view of them, as they entered the building. Each of them took a seat at a small table, one dropping her head into her hands while the other two looked both morose and hopeless.

Hopeless? Guardian angels weren't allowed to look hopeless. No angels were allowed to ever look hopeless. There was no such thing within the Heavenly realms. Angels were supposed to inspire, bring about hope, and encourage humans to have faith; never give up or wallow in despair.

Sighing, Matthias stood to his full height and moved in their direction. It was time to fulfill his responsibilities. He was in charge of training the newer guardian angels. He entered the small schoolroom and then stopped a few feet away from the three.

"What are you three angels doing?" Matthias asked. "The celebration is about to begin."

When none of them offered an answer to his question, he crossed his arms over his chest and made a noise letting them know his patience wasn't everlasting.

Young angels in training could be considered quite troublesome by some of the older angels, but Matthias had willingly embraced taking the youngsters under his wings and helping them become the very best guardian angels they could be. This was his second year supervising this particular trio of angels. He knew better than to let them congregate and share their woes with one another. In the past, that had led to them giving one another advice, most of which violated the angel code and had forced him to intervene and correct the resulting situations. He did not look forward to repeating those experiences this Christmas season.

He cleared his throat to gain their attention and then met their eyes, one by one. "Well?"

"My little boy is so sad," Joy told him, dramatically tossing her hands out to her sides.

Joy was just beginning her second year of guardian angel training. She had struggled with several of her assignments in the past twelve months. In order to graduate from the guardian angel school, the little angels were given a variety of special assignments. All three of these angels had failed their special assignments the year before and were being given another chance to fulfill their duties without interfering in ways that were off-limits.

Humans were complex creatures with a God-given free will. While the angels could help facilitate opportunities, they weren't allowed to force or coerce their charges to do the prudent and correct thing. Joy had forgotten that fact the year before when she had played upon her charge's emotions in order to get them to follow a certain path. Unfortunately for Joy, human emotions were very volatile. Soon enough, her charge realized she had been manipulated but had blamed that fact upon a close family member, not where the blame had truly belonged—on her guardian angel.

Matthias had removed Joy from her guardianship of that human and had spent the next two months helping to bring about a reconciliation between the two humans; all because of the misconception that had arisen by Joy's overstep. Explaining the situation to the Archangel who oversaw the entire guardian angel program had been even worse. Matthias never wanted to go through that experience again.

Matthias nodded in acknowledgement of her response and then looked to the next angel. "And you, Hope? The last time we talked you were excited about your current assignment."

"My charge doesn't even want to celebrate Christmas this

year," Hope stated, huffing out a breath, as she dropped her chin into her cupped hands. "How can anyone not want to celebrate Christmas? It's not…well, it's just not right. Or human. They love Christmas and their made-up celebratory figures. The snowman who danced and sang…"

"…and then melted when the sun came out," Matthias told her with a small smile.

"I'm talking about before that. And humans love the story of the little reindeer whose nose glowed and could fly. That story had a happy ending."

"But the idea behind Christmas has nothing to do with those things," Matthias reminded her needlessly.

"I know that." Hope nodded and added, "But my charge's file states that she loved all of those things until a year ago. Now, she abhors the very idea of Christmas. I'm trying not to hold that against her, but I must confess; it's very hard. Christmas is the most wonderful time of the year, but my charge hates it."

"Well, at least your charge doesn't visit the cemetery every day. It's really sad to watch her cry—day after day—and not even try to go on living her life," Charity added.

Charity was the most mature of the angels in training and had already successfully completed two of the three special assignments. If she was successful in helping her current charge overcome a soul-searing grief, she would graduate at the end of January.

Matthias looked at the three and shook his head, "So you three are just going to sit around up here moaning about your difficult situations rather than try to find a solution to them?"

Joy looked up at him. "What are we supposed to do? I mean, it's only a few weeks before Christmas. How are people supposed to remember they're celebrating the birth of the Christ Child if they are so unhappy?"

Matthias grinned. "You find a way to make them happy. Help them remember the good things in life and give them hope which is what Christmas is all about. Your job is to try to get your charges to see that. Remember...a guardian angel doesn't just keep their charge from getting run over as they cross the street; you also have to help your charge in the emotional, spiritual, and mental realm."

The three angels looked at each other. Their expressions slowly started to change. Hope was the first to speak.

"I could help Claire want to celebrate Christmas."

"And I could help Maddie find another outlet for her grief," added Charity. "What about you, Joy? Why is your little boy so sad?"

Joy was happy that her friends were coming up with solutions. Maybe they could help her brainstorm a solution to her little charge's request. While the other two angels had been assigned adult charges, Joy had been assigned to watch over a little boy. She'd considered herself the luckiest of the three when they'd been given their assignments. Now, she wasn't so sure. "My little boy wants his mama not to be so sad. She's lonely. He wants to help her but doesn't know how."

"Maybe she needs a puppy to love?" Hope suggested with a smile.

"Puppies are nice. So are kittens," Charity offered. "This time of year, there are always an abundance at the animal shelters. Maybe your little charge's mother could adopt a new pet?"

Joy appreciated their help, but she didn't think either of their answers were going to help Sam, her charge. Puppies and kittens took a lot of energy. After watching them, Sam's mother lacked extra energy at this time.

Matthias squatted down so that he was eye-level with the littlest of the three angels. "You'll find a way. I have faith in you."

9

"Thanks?" Joy queried, wishing she had as much faith in herself, as the head of the angel school seemed to have. "Maybe we should brainstorm more ideas…"

Matthias shook his head, "That is not going to happen while I'm around. I'm still recovering from the last brainstorming session you three had together. If you need to bounce ideas off of someone, I am always available to you."

Joy gave him a sheepish look and then snuck a glance at her two companions, noticing that they also looked embarrassed and were trying to avoid Matthias' searing glance. She decided it was up to her to put Matthias in a better mood. She offered him a small smile. "I guess I should probably get back down there, huh?"

"That would be a good place to start," Matthias agreed with a nod and warm smile. "You should all be busy trying to help your charges right now. Christmas is only two weeks away. You all should know better than anyone just how fast time can fly. Go and tend to your charges and remember; I am always here if you need advice or just to talk through a plan."

Hope, Charity and Joy nodded dutifully, and each said, "Thank you."

Matthias smiled at each of them. "Off with you all now. Go enjoy the celebration for a bit and then take that enthusiasm back to your duties. We'll have even more to celebrate once you three have your charges sorted out."

Joy looked at her friends. They all silently agreed. They were going to help their charges, whether those charges wanted to be helped right now or not. Their charges would never know why their situations had changed. The angels would have to comply with the rules and regulations for interactions with their humans. They would need to keep in mind; where there was a will, there was always a way.

10

her desk. Sam was oblivious to the presence of his guardian angel, hovering just behind him, as she kept watch over her young charge. He was slightly out of breath, but that didn't dampen his enthusiasm one bit.

"Mom. I'm here. Can we go to the park now?" He wiggled his arms and allowed his backpack to drop with a dull thud to the floor.

Melissa Bartell looked up from the paper she'd been studying and forced a smile to her lips.

"Hey, little man. How was school?" She opened her arms and the little boy rushed into them, hugged her briefly and then danced away again, unable to stay still for even a few seconds.

"School was good. Can we go now?" Sam asked, hopping from foot to foot and twirling toward the large windows in the office that overlooked the city below.

"You saw that it was snowing outside, right?" Melissa asked, as she got up from her desk and joined her son at the windows. When her cell phone beeped, reminding her that she was running late for a meeting, she reached for the coat she'd discarded an hour earlier. "Sure you want to go hang out in a city park covered in snow instead of at home where it's nice and warm?"

"Yeah." Sam rolled his eyes at the same time he nodded his head while adding, "I have my hat and my gloves." He held up the gloves and then waved his stocking hat in the air for her to see.

Melissa tousled his hair and then smiled down at him. "Okay, I guess I can stress while walking through the park as well as I can stress sitting here. Let's go."

Sam frowned at his mother's comments and Joy leaned closer, wondering what was bothering the beautiful young mother. It was easy to see where Sam got his coloring from, his mother's long blonde tresses had streaks of gold and a blonde that was so light it was a shimmery white mixed throughout. Her gray eyes matched Sam's, as did the small dimple that appeared in her cheek as it did in Sam's whenever he was happy and smiling; behaviors that happened far too seldom in recent days for Joy's liking.

"Why are you stressing?" Sam asked, taking his mother's gloved hand, as they left her office and took the elevator down to the ground floor. His mother nodded at Jim as they exited the building and began the short walk to the city park. There was a slight breeze, but Sam didn't even feel the cold. He was waiting on his mother for an answer to his question.

Melissa glanced down at him and made a silly face, "It's been a bad—very bad—day."

Sam pursed his lips at her reference to one of his favorite books; *Alexander and the Terrible, Horrible, No Good, Very Bad Day*.

He highly doubted his mother was capable of having such a day, but then again, being an adult seemed like lots of work and very little fun. He stepped a little closer to her and then nodded and pursed his lips in a bad imitation of the look she always gave him in such a situation. "So, tell me all about it."

Melissa chuckled and shook her head at his silliness. "Where have I heard that before?"

"You. It's what you always tell me when I've had a bad day. I'm all ears, mom."

Melissa shook her head again and laid a hand on his jacketed shoulder, "Thanks, sweetie, but you don't need to worry about my problems."

"Mom! You always say we're a team of two." Sam danced away from her and turned around so that he was walking backwards and threw his arms out to the side. "You talk and I'll listen."

Melissa raised a brow at her son and then spun him around, so he wouldn't stumble and fall into the street. "I've heard that before, as well." She winked at him and then explained the most pressing issue on her mind. "So, I got a phone call earlier this afternoon. It seems there was an accident and the Christmas trees aren't coming," she told him, keeping her eyes straight ahead. She tried to push aside the panic saying the words aloud had created.

A Christmas Festival without Christmas trees? Who had ever heard of such a thing? If the festival wasn't a success this year... People from all over the Denver area come to visit the festival with the intention of purchasing their Christmas tree at the end of the outing. Once word gets out that there are no Christmas trees this year, will anyone even bother to drive across town?

Sam stopped walking, pulling on his mother's hand to gain her attention. "The Christmas trees aren't coming? But...but the Christmas trees...you can't have a Christmas festival without Christmas trees."

Melissa nodded sadly and squatted down, so she was on eye-level with Sam. "I agree, buddy. However, this close to Christmas, there's not enough time to find another supplier to haul them out here. Besides, the two Christmas tree farms I called this afternoon don't have enough trees or manpower to harvest the trees they have left. I don't know what I'm going to do. I've kind of exhausted my available options."

Sam nodded, as Melissa stood back up, and they continued walking. His little expression was still far too serious, as they entered the park. Almost immediately, his mother was snagged by a vendor who had questions. Sam knew it would be quite a while before his mother made her way to the center tent and impatience won out.

"I'm going to the nativity scene, mom," Sam called out even as he was walking away.

"Sam, stay where I can see you. Okay?" Melissa called out after him. The nativity scene was just a few dozen yards away from the event tent and easily seen from their present location.

"I will." Sam waved and took off, making sure he walked through the fresh snow and left his mark upon the landscape.

The city park where the festival was being held sat between the Museum of Natural History and the Denver Zoo. It was a large property and included a small golf course which was now closed due to the inclement weather. Melissa was only utilizing one small corner of the park for the Christmas Festival. In the distance, one could see the warning fence that had been erected to keep festival attendees from wandering onto the golf course.

The year before, a group of teenagers had wandered onto the golf course during the Christmas Festival and had vandalized the caddy shack before anyone had realized what was happening. The damages had been small, but the city manager had blamed Melissa for not having foreseen that such a thing might happen. Melissa had assured him that additional precautions would be taken this year. She could only cross her fingers as the opening of the festival neared and pray that they wouldn't have any incidences. Too much was riding on the festival being successful this year.

Melissa finally broke free from the vendors and headed for her makeshift headquarters here at City Park. Several large pressurized domes had already been set up where vendors could sell their wares and where she and her staff would oversee and manage the festival. Hot air kept the domes inflated and also warmed the air inside, making them a pleasant escape from the chilly weather outside. This was a new amenity being offered this year. Melissa was hopeful it would bring more people out in attendance.

Her assistant met her with a stack of messages. Melissa inwardly cringed when she saw more than half of them were from the last man she wanted to deal with today. The city manager. She tucked

16

the messages from him to the back of the pile, ignoring the knowing smile her assistant sent her way, and then headed for her makeshift desk. With any luck, she wouldn't have any more problems heaped on her shoulders. She needed a chance to figure out the tree situation and several other pressing concerns before she could handle even one more issue.

***

Sam reached the nativity scene and quickly slipped over the railing and sat down by the manger. This is where he'd been coming for the last week and, like those other times, he began speaking to the fake infant, telling it all about his mother's unhappiness and how he didn't need anything for Christmas; he just wanted his mother to be happy.

"Baby Jesus, Christmas is only a few weeks away. I don't need anything for myself, but please bring mama a husband. Maybe if she wasn't so lonely, she'd be happy again. I looked at school today, but I didn't find anyone who didn't already have a mama and a daddy. It makes mama sad when she comes to my school plays. She has to sit all by herself."

Sam grew quiet for a moment and then he added another request. "Mama's real sad about the Christmas trees. Could you maybe send her some of them, too? My friends all went and talked to the guy in the Santa suit at the mall, but I told them that was just silly. Mrs. Barnes taught us in Sunday school that Jesus has all the answers to our problems. That's why I'm talking to You about this."

He looked up at the winter sky and then glanced back at the plastic baby. "I know there's lots of people in the world with big problems, but maybe…if it's not too much to ask, you could answer mine?"

"Sam!" his mother's voice carried over the crisp air.

"I gotta go, but I'll be back tomorrow. Thanks for helping my mama." Sam got to his feet and climbed over the railing. He waved to his mother and rushed to where she was patiently waiting. When he reached her side, he announced, "I'm hungry." side.

She chuckled and nodded. "Tell me something new. How about we stop and grab a pizza before heading home?"

"Yes!" Sam agreed, as he raised a fist in the air. Pizza was his all-time favorite food.

****

Joy watched as mother and son headed for her vehicle, parked only a block away. A plan was already beginning to form for how to deal with Sam's unhappiness and his latest request. This was the first time Sam had actually mentioned what he thought might make his mama happy. A husband.

That immediately got Joy thinking. She was almost giddy at the idea of playing matchmaker. She'd have to follow the rules, which meant she couldn't toy with anyone's emotions. After last year's debacle, she'd promised Matthias to stick to the guardian angel code, but making sure Melissa Bartell had an opportunity to meet an eligible man wasn't in that book of codes. Melissa hadn't know that she should've been dreaming about a certain eligible man all these months.

Joy had been watching the request board which angels used to help one another do their jobs more efficiently. Just yesterday, a fellow angel had posted about her charge who was discouraged because he hadn't been able to find a buyer for his trees. The man had started his own Christmas tree farm a number of years earlier and was finally ready to start selling them, but a series of events had prevented him from harvesting them earlier. Now, he couldn't find anyone nearby to purchase them. The man's location was less than two hours away from Denver. To Joy, this situation was tailor-made in heaven. She wasn't about to let this opportunity slip away.

Joy immediately sent out a request and headed off to meet the other angel. To set things in motion, she needed a business card to fall into Sam's mom's hands. With the Christmas tree situation taken care of, now she only needed to find Sam's mom a husband. Compared to some of the other tasks she'd performed, this one should be a piece of cake...make that a Christmas yule log. It was the holiday season, after all.

Chapter 2

Two days later…

"Melissa, the guy from the tree farm is here," Sandy James called up the ladder to where her boss—the person in charge of making the Christmas Festival a success—was currently trying to untangle a string of lights. Why one of the city maintenance workers wasn't up on the ladder was unclear at the moment.

"Just a minute," a voice answered back, as the ladder started wobbling dangerously.

"Whoa!" Sandy lunged forward to stabilize the ladder just as another body pushed her out of the way and grabbed the ladder with big hands.

"I've got this," a deep tenor voice floated up to the top of the ladder. Melissa looked down into the bluest eyes she'd ever seen. "You okay up there?"

Melissa nodded and then blushed when she remembered he could only see the lower half of her since her head was partially concealed behind the festival's sign. Taking a calming breath, she called back down, "I'm fine. I'm coming down right now."

She descended the ladder, pausing when she reached the point where the stranger was holding it steady.

"Thank you," she murmured, as he stepped back, so she climbed the rest of the way down. She dusted off her hands and then looked past the stranger to where Sandy stood patiently waiting. She looked to Sandy's right and then gave the stranger a cursory glance. She wasn't sure who he was, but he was handsome, dressed in a red plaid flannel jacket with a hoodie pulled up over his hair. She briefly wondered what his hair looked like, but she quickly dismissed her wayward thoughts, bringing them back to the present. She didn't have time in her life for anything more than a fleeting second of appreciation for a handsome man—and this man definitely fit that category.

He appeared to be giving her appearance a thorough once-over as well. Melissa met his eyes briefly once more and then turned away, as she felt a blush creep into her cheeks. She didn't have time for…whatever, this was. There was no denying the man was gorgeous and exactly the type of man Melissa would be attracted to, if she ever gave herself permission to go down that road again. She currently didn't have time or the inclination for any sort of relationship if it didn't involve work and the festival. She most definitely didn't have time to nurse a broken heart. In her experience, heartbreak was the only thing at the end of the road when dealing with a handsome man. No, thank you.

She looked back at Sandy with a raised brow, "You said the guy from the tree farm was here. Where is he?"

She'd only spoken to the man on the phone a few times. She'd been expecting an older gentleman, possibly with greying or even white hair. His voice had been gravelly, and she'd pictured a slimmer version of Santa. Her imagination had placed him sitting in a rocking chair with a pipe in one hand, as he talked to her about his Christmas trees on the phone with the other. She didn't see anyone fitting that description nearby.

Sandy bit her bottom lip and then pointed unobtrusively at the stranger. Melissa turned her head and made eye contact with the handsome man. He nodded and stuck out his hand. She took it, ignoring how warm it was and how strong it felt.

"I would be the guy with the Christmas trees."

She ignored the way his deep blue eyes seemed to sparkle with mirth and forced herself to act professional. "Sorry. I'm Melissa Bartell, Community Events Director, and this is my assistant Sandy

James. I was expecting…" She broke off, as she realized how rude her assumptions might seem if she were to give voice to them.

"Sandy and I already met," his deep voice reverberated inside her chest, and a feeling of warmth surrounded her. He shook her hand and the feeling of warmth flowed up her arm. "Jarod Gregory. Christmas Valley Pines." He looked around and then offered her a smile. "This is no small undertaking you have going on here."

Melissa smiled back, his comment helping her focus on the reason he was standing before her. "This is my fifth year running the festival. Each year, it seems to get more complicated than the last. Before I forget, thank you so much for stepping in at the last minute. The Christmas tree supplier we've used for the last few years hit a patch of ice coming through Idaho and their trailer overturned."

Jarod looked concerned. "Was anyone injured?"

"Only the four hundred trees he was carrying. Actually, I spoke to him a few days ago. He said quite a few of the trees remained undamaged, but his tractor trailer didn't fare as well. With it being so close to the holidays, he couldn't find another way to transport the trees out here until the twentieth of December which is a few days before the festival ends."

"Without the draw of the Christmas trees, we wouldn't get nearly as many people to attend the festival," Sandy interjected, moving forward into their small circle. "The city council is looking for ways to save money. This festival has been on their hatchet list for the last two years. If attendance was to suddenly drop, they would cut us out of next year's budget in a heartbeat."

Jarod nodded his understanding and then looked around for a moment before turning back to the conversation. "Well, I'm happy I could help."

"Let's go this way, and I'll show you what we have designated for the tree lot," Melissa told him, turning and walking toward the opposite side of the area cordoned off for the festival.

"This is actually the first year I've had trees to sell," Jarod informed her, "I inherited the land from my grandfather and moved out here from Oregon almost seven years ago now. My parents have a big tree farm back there and provided me the seedlings needed to start one here, but it takes years before a new operation is ready to do more than tend the trees." Jarod walked by her side, his long legs eating up the distance, but he walked at a leisurely pace, so Melissa was impressed that she never once felt as if she was having to hurry to keep up with him.

Melissa veered to her right and they began to cut across the center of the park. "Seven years is a long time to do nothing but watch trees grow. I had to admit I was actually shocked to find that there was someone in that area of the state who was growing trees. The pine beetles have all but decimated the national forests around here."

Jarod made a sound of agreement. "I noticed that when I first came out here. We have the same thing back in Oregon, so I was prepared for how to protect my farm. I spray the trees in early May and then make sure they're getting enough fertilizer and water throughout the growing season. Healthy trees don't seem to be the beetle's natural habitat, so I do my best to make sure mine are the healthiest in the county. So far, I haven't had any trees get infected."

"Well, I hope you don't. Let me show you where you'll be setting up. There's already a fence around the area with lights and such."

Melissa led him past the life-sized nativity scene, halting her forward progress when she spied her son inside the scene, kneeling next to the manger and the figure of baby Jesus. She saw his lips move, as he carried on a one-sided conversation with the infant and sighed. Sam had seemed so down this holiday Season, and he'd been insistent on coming to the park with her each afternoon when school was out. He didn't seem interested in the exhibits being set up, except for one; the nativity scene.

Jarod nodded his head toward Sam and asked, "Someone you know?"

"My son," she told him with a small turn of her lips.

"He seems to be having quite the conversation over there," Jarod pointed out.

Melissa nodded, "A daily occurrence, I assure you." She stepped forward and called out, "Sam."

Her son turned his head and then waved. She waved back and gestured for him to join her, smiling when he picked up his backpack and ran to her. She bent down and hugged him when he got there, "Hey. I thought maybe you'd like to go see the Christmas trees."

Sam's eyes widened, and he looked at Jarod, "Did he bring them?"

Melissa nodded, "He did. On a big truck?" she guessed, looking to Jarod for confirmation.

"On a big truck. You look like you're pretty smart. You interested in helping me out for a little bit?" Jarod asked, earning a grin from Sam and a curious look from Melissa.

"What kind of help are we talking about?" Melissa asked.

"Well, I need to keep track of the trees as they're unloaded. I brought a couple of high school guys with me to get the stands on and everything unloaded, but I could sure use someone to help keep track of things. You can count, can't you?" Jarod asked with a smirk he barely managed to contain.

Sam stood up tall and nodded, "I can count really high. My teacher says I'm excst...excert...."

He looked at Melissa, and she provided the word he was

looking for, "Exceptional."

Sam grinned, "Yeah. Exceptional. I'm exceptional at math."

"Great. You're the man I need."

Melissa shook her head as Sam took off sprinting across the snow-covered expanse of lawn, "I hope you know what you just signed up for."

"I have two nephews and three nieces," Jarod informed her. "I've missed them, and Sam seems like a great kid."

Melissa nodded, "He is."

They reached the fenced space, and she asked, "What do you think? Will this be enough room?"

Jarod looked around and then nodded. "Plenty. I'd better get things rolling here, so we can get unloaded before dark. Your assistant mentioned something about the festival opening a day early?"

Melissa gave him an apologetic look, "Yeah. Sorry I didn't have a chance to let you know. They're forecasting a big storm tomorrow and most of the vendors are ready to go so we're doing a soft open tonight. We'll open at six o'clock. Any chance you might be ready to sell trees by then? So many people wait to purchase their Christmas tree from the lot here…there'll be a lot of disappointed people if they have to go somewhere else."

Sam came running back to them, a giddy smile spread across his little face. "Mom! You should see all of the trees. Oodles and oodles of them."

"I hope so, we have oodles and oodles of people coming to buy them. About tonight?" she asked Jarod hesitantly.

"We'll be ready. After all, I have an exceptional counter ready to help out."

Jarod bumped gloved knuckles with Sam. She felt a pain in her heart. She'd married his father right out of college and had thought they were on the same page where their family was concerned. Sam's dad had left almost immediately after Melissa had told him he was going to be a father. He'd told her he wasn't ready to be tied down to a kid and, when she'd refused to even consider an abortion, he'd filed for a quick divorce and moved to California.

Melissa had been so excited about the prospect of becoming a mom, she hadn't even thought about fighting Tyler over the divorce or asking for child support. He'd made it clear he wanted nothing to do with his child. Melissa had petitioned the court to go back to using her maiden name. She'd given it to Sam when he was born and listed his father on the birth certificate, but that had been where Tyler Jamison's connection to her son ended.

As Sam had gotten older, she'd been struggling with a sense of guilt that he didn't have a man in his life to help guide him through the coming years. Sam was in second grade now. He was also the only child in his class that didn't have at least one father figure in his life. Her own parents were no longer around to help out. It was just her and Sam.

Some days, it was all she could do to get through the day by telling herself that tomorrow would be better. Tomorrow, she wouldn't feel lonely. Tomorrow, she'd find someone to confide in that didn't wear *Teenage Mutant Ninja Turtle* pajamas to bed. Tomorrow...

"Mom?" Sam was tugging on the hem of her coat.

"What?" she looked down and realized she'd let her mind drift. "Oh, Sam. I'm sorry. Lots of things on my mind this time of year. Are you okay sticking around and helping Mr. Gregory with the trees?"

"Sure. I count things really good."

"I know you do," she touched his shoulder for a brief moment and then took a step back. "I'll let you boys get to it, then. Sam, I'll be over at the event tent. When you're done helping Mr. Gregory, you come find me. Okay?"

"Okay," Sam readily agreed, dismissing her and starting up a conversation with Jarod right away.

Melissa watched for a long moment, pushing aside the guilt and unhappiness that always crept in whenever she thought of her fatherless son. She was doing the best she could, but the holidays were always hard. On both of them.

As she headed back to tackle the next item on her to-do list, she made a mental note to check out the local Boys and Girls Club right after the first of the year. Sam needed a male role model in his life. She'd heard from several people about the Big Brother program and how well it was doing. She couldn't make Sam's dad acknowledge his existence, but maybe she could find someone who would pay attention to Sam and help him grow into a fine young man. Someone who might be willing to teach him what being a real man was all about and answer the questions she knew he would have in the future but might not feel comfortable talking to her about.

"Sandy," she called out, as she entered the tent. "Did this evening's entertainment show up yet?"

"They just arrived."

Melissa nodded, glad that the local rock band had been willing and able to fill the stage on a moment's notice. They were popular amongst the younger population, and she was hoping that would draw a younger demographic out to the festival. "Anything else pressing right now?"

"You and a cup of hot chocolate," Sandy informed her, handing her a covered cup and turning her toward her makeshift office. "Go kick your feet up for five minutes."

"But…," Melissa took the cup and a few steps forward, but then she remembered the list of items she still needed to deal with.

"I promise none of your problems are going to go away in the next five minutes." Sandy gave her a look with one raised brow, daring her to argue. "You know I'm right."

"As always. Fine, but only for five minutes." She took the hot chocolate, sipping it as she sat down and leaned back in the chair. She tried to clear her brain, but that only allowed the image of the Christmas tree man to intrude. He was handsome…but, she couldn't allow herself to be swayed by that. Nor could she spend time wondering why walking beside him had felt so…right.

Had I ever felt like that with Sam's dad?

Realizing where her thoughts were headed, she sat up and pushed the unfinished cup of hot chocolate away. No, she had a job to do. It was time to focus on the festival now. The past wasn't something she would change. The present day demanded she do her best to ensure the thousands of people who would be arriving later today had a memorable experience. Her personal problems would just have to wait.

Chapter 3

Guardian Angel School

Heaven

"Joy, you look rather pleased with yourself," Matthias commented, as he stepped into the angel lounge. He hadn't seen Joy or the other little angels for several days and was curious to know if she'd come up with any strategies yet.

Joy gave him a big smile and nodded. "That's because I'm well on my way to solving my charge's unhappiness."

"Really? Do tell," Matthias offered. He figured it was better to know if she was planning to break any rules right up front. Perhaps, he could prevent a repeat of last year's disaster. "I assume you figured out what was making him so unhappy?"

"I did."

When she didn't immediately elaborate, Matthias tried to hide his concern and leaned forward. "And?"

"Well…he was unhappy because his mother is so lonely. He asked the fake baby Jesus in a nativity scene to find his mama a husband, so she could be happy at Christmas. Then, there was an accident, and the Christmas trees got tipped over, and he was sad because they can't have a Christmas festival without Christmas trees…and…" Joy stopped talking and looked up. "Don't you see? Everything is working out."

Matthias grinned. Joy had a tendency to talk rapidly, running all her sentences together when she got excited. After being around her for more than a year, he could finally *almost* decipher what she was trying to communicate without too much trouble. In this instance, he needed more details, especially since she was convinced everything was *working out*. That could either be really good or signal the beginning of a problem. Better to deal with it right now

29

than be surprised later.

"I might need a bit more explanation before I can see how *everything is working out* with what you just told me. Maybe you should slow down and explain how an accident and Christmas trees tipping over are to be considered good things?"

Joy blinked and then smiled, "Oh, I forgot some parts. The Christmas trees for the festival were in an accident. The tractor trailer truck carrying them tipped over. Sam's mother, Melissa, couldn't find any other trees to replace them. That made Sam very sad. I saw something on the help board about a tree farmer who had no place to sell his trees, so I made sure Melissa found his phone number."

She was grinning from ear to ear and bouncing a bit with excitement over the next part of her story. "The man who owns the tree farm? Well, he's very handsome and single and just as lonely as Sam's mother."

Matthias's grin faded as he jumped ahead to the reason the little angel seemed to be so excited. "Joy, you know angels are not allowed to influence the emotions of humans."

"I know that, but it can't be a coincidence that the answer to the tree problem came in the form of a nice single man, can it?"

Matthias took a breath and then issued a soft warning, "Just be careful. You've introduced them to one another. That is all you can do."

Joy made a circle with the thumb and forefinger of each hand and then interlocked them. "Angel promise."

Smiling, Matthias nodded. "Good. That's what I like to hear."

Joy watched him move away and then headed back down to see how things were going with her charge. She was very excited to see how things were going to work out for Sam and his mother. There were only two weeks until Christmas, but this was the Season of miracles. Even angels believed in the magic of Christmas.

***

Denver, Colorado

"Jarod, do you need anything else from us?" Mitch Ellers hollered across the tree lot. Mitch had turned eighteen several months earlier and would be graduating from high school in May. He and several of the other high school boys had been working part-time for Jarod for almost a year now and had jumped at the chance to miss a few days of school in order to help transport the Christmas trees over to Denver.

Mitch had completed and passed his commercial driver's license and could now legally drive the truck used to transport the trees. His license wouldn't allow him to drive the trees outside Colorado, but Jarod had no intention of trying to sell his trees anywhere but within a few hours of the farm.

Jarod looked around at the dozens of trees that had been placed in the fenced area, the multi-colored lights that had been strung overhead reflected off the piles of snow at the edges of the tree lot, giving the trees the appearance of being adorned with brightly colored flashes of light. He smiled and then stretched his sore muscles, evidence of a day of hard work. His dream of having his own Christmas tree operation had finally reached the final stage—selling the trees to the public.

He looked back at the young man who had worked just as hard as he had and shook his head. "I can't think of anything else that needs done. You and Deke head on over to the hotel but be back around 5:30. The festival opens at 6:00."

"Will do. You want us to bring you some dinner?" Mitch called back.

"Nah. I'll get something from one of the vendors here a bit later." He watched the two high school boys head for their truck, now

31

minus the large flatbed where the trees had been stacked, and then turned back to see Sam still hard at work. The little boy was counting up all of the trees, his brow furrowed in concentration as he chewed on the end of a pencil and his lips moved silently along with his fingers as he performed a calculation. Jarod wandered over and stopped a few feet in front of Sam.

"Did we miss any?"

Sam finished his count and then shook his head, "Nope. I counted 'em twice and there are one hundred and fifty Douglas Firs, sixty-five Noble Firs under eight feet tall and thirty that are nine feet or taller, and one hundred and twenty Grand Firs. That's a total of…three hundred and sixty-five trees."

"Oh, good. That's the exact number of trees we cut down and loaded onto the truck," Jarod told him. "I'm happy to know that we didn't lose any of them on the trek here. Ready to go find your mom?"

Sam nodded and placed the clipboard down on the table, "Do you think maybe I could come back here?"

"Hey, if it's okay with your mom, it's fine by me. You really were a lot of help today."

"Thanks. Mitch and Deke were cool. Mitch said he'd give me some more football pointers tomorrow, if it's okay with you and my mom."

Jarod hid his smile at the way Sam was trying so hard to be older than his young years. He hadn't missed the way the young boy's eyes had followed the two high schoolers around, and when they'd taken a short break to toss a football around, he'd seen Sam's eyes light up. They'd patiently included him and made sure he was able to catch the passes they tossed his way. He'd been reminded of his nephews and nieces once again and made a mental note to call and check in with them soon.

"Mitch and Deke were a lot of help today. Just like you were. Come on. Your mom's probably wondering what's taking us so long."

"She's probably still dealing with one problem or another. She's good at that."

"Dealing with problems?" Jarod inquired while Sam pulled his gloves back on.

Sam nodded, "This time of year she has a lot of them. Everyone brings their problems to her, and it's her job to fix things. She's kind of like a bottle of Elmer's glue."

Jarod squinted in confusion. "Your mother is a bottle of white school glue?"

Sam nodded and giggled, "She fixes all sorts of things, but don't tell her I called her glue. She might not think that was very nice."

Jarod pretended to lock his lips and toss away the key. "I won't say a word."

He barely hid his smile until Sam had gone ahead of him and then he gave way to the urge and shook his head. The unpredictable comments that came out of children's mouths was one of the things he missed most about his nephews. No filters. No trying to be politically correct. Just the facts the way a child saw them. Black and white. Big. Bold. Sometimes, a truth right in your face that you couldn't deny.

They headed back to the large red and white tent that had been erected in the middle of the park. They were more than halfway there when Sam stopped. "I need to do something before we go find my mom."

"What?" Jarod asked in a puzzled voice.

"I need to go to the nativity. You don't have to go with me, if you don't want," Sam offered. "I'll just be a minute."

"No," Jarod shrugged, "I wouldn't mind seeing it a little closer up. Lead the way."

He watched as Sam took off, his little legs eating up the ground, as he hurried towards the manger scene; complete with barn animals, wise men, and life-sized camels. Jarod strolled behind him, admiring the craftsmanship that had gone into carving each figure. They appeared to not only be hand-carved, but hand-painted. Jarod was impressed by the intricacy of the display.

He was examining one of the camels when Sam's little voice wafted over the air.

"You won't believe what's happened. We have Christmas trees. Mama smiled a bit, but she's still lonely. She's unhappy. I heard her crying again last night. She was asking for your help...er, well...she was asking for God's help, but you can get a message to him, can't you. Anyway, I know you can, so here I am, asking for your help again. Help mama smile again and give her someone to talk to after I go to bed."

Jarod stepped closer, not quite sure if Sam was talking about his mother or someone else but hearing that she'd been crying concerned him. Throughout the day Sam had talked his ear off. He'd talked about school. His friends. His mom. His pet turtle named Leonardo.

Jarod was proud of himself for recognizing the reference to the popular children's show depicting mutated turtles and a sewer rat that used martial arts to fight evil. Sam had been genuinely shocked that Jarod knew who he was talking about and the fact that he wore the blue mask and carried two short swords.

Sam had explained how he'd gone as Leonardo for Halloween, but his mother had refused to buy him authentic swords. Instead, she'd found some foam replicas at a local dollar store. She'd explained that it was her sole responsibility to keep him safe which she couldn't do if he was walking around the neighborhood with two swords that could cut someone.

Jarod had made appropriate responses, getting another glimpse into the workings of Sam's mind when the boy confessed about hiding them in his desk at school, so the other kids wouldn't laugh at him. After all, Tommy Vanderhaven had brought real nunchakus to go with his Michelangelo costume; the one with the orange mask. In Sam's mind, it didn't matter that Tommy had been called into the principal's office and been forced to leave the nunchakus there until his parents came to pick him up. Nothing seemed to trump the fact that Tommy had brought real ninja weapons to school instead of fake ones.

Through all of his conversations, he'd never mentioned a dad or any other relatives which Jarod found strange. His own nephews constantly talked about both of their parents and their relatives. Listening to Sam holding his one-sided conversation with the nativity infant sparked his curiosity about Melissa and her situation. He hadn't missed the dark circles beneath her eyes, or the momentary look of sadness in her eyes when she'd looked at Sam sitting in the nativity scene. All was not right in the young woman's world. Jarod had a sudden desire to do what he could to try and fix things.

He told himself it had nothing to do with how gorgeous she was or the fact that his palm had tingled when he'd shaken her hand. It wasn't a reaction he'd been expecting, and it had taken a lot for him to focus on his reason for being in Denver. He blamed his slight interest on one of his few character flaws. The same flaw that had gotten him into trouble more than once. He just couldn't see anyone in need, especially a bright, beautiful young woman, and not do whatever he could to fix her problems.

This time, something was different. Normally, he would jump in and help solve whatever problem was currently present and then go on about his business. Something about the gorgeous Melissa told him that he wouldn't want to walk away if he allowed himself to get involved with her. He told himself he was just here to sell trees, but his thought sounded lame even in his own mind. Jarod had met lots of beautiful women, but Melissa was the first one who had grabbed his attention from the moment he'd seen her.

A few minutes later, Sam climbed back over the railing. "I'm done."

Jarod glanced down at the little boy and nodded. "I heard you talking to the baby statue."

"Baby Jesus. I know he's not real, but that doesn't matter. Does it?" Sam asked, the confidence in his voice faltering slightly.

"No, it doesn't matter. Jesus can hear you anywhere and anytime you choose to talk to him."

Sam visibly relaxed and grinned, "That's what Mrs. Barnes always tells us."

"Who is Mrs. Barnes?" Jarod asked.

"My Sunday School teacher. She's been teaching Sunday School for a really, really long time. She has white hair, and she always smells kind of funny, but she tells us Bible stories and even prays for us. And she brings us cupcakes."

Jarod smiled, remembering a Sunday School teacher from his past that seemed to have been cut from the same cloth. "Sunday School teachers are amazing. Mine was named Mrs. Traverton. She was like a grandmother to me. She liked to sing songs."

Sam looked up at him, "I don't have one of those."

"A grandmother?" Jarod asked.

Sam nodded. "I don't have a dad either."

Jarod was even more concerned to hear Sam talk as if he and

his mother were all alone in the world. He had so much extended family, he couldn't imagine having no one else.

"Does that make you sad?' Jarod asked quietly.

"Not me, but I think it makes mama sad some. Do you remember the songs your Sunday School teacher liked to sing?" Sam had the uncanny ability of a child to switch subjects like the wind changed directions.

Jarod thought for a moment and then nodded. "I remember a few. There was one about Father Abraham and had all of these funny motions we did while we were singing. What about you? Does your Sunday School teacher like to sing songs?"

Sam shook his head and made a funny face. "No and we don't want her to. I know it's not very nice to say, but Mrs. Barnes sounds like a sick cow when she tries to sing. She said she had a voice only God could love and, out of respect for our ears, she was going to stay quiet."

Jarod laughed aloud, unable to stop himself. "Sorry, Sam."

"Don't be." The little boy joined in his laughter. "Mrs. Barnes looks really funny when she tries to sing as well. I try not to laugh cuz I don't want to hurt her feelings or nothin'."

"I'm sure she appreciates that." Jarod looked up when he heard someone call Sam's name and watched as Melissa made her way towards them.

"There's your mom."

"I was just coming to get him, so you didn't have to bring him back," she told Jarod when she was a few feet away from them.

"No problem. We finished up a few minutes ago, but he wanted to stop by the nativity scene."

"He's fascinated with it this year," she told him.

"He was talking to the Baby Jesus replica," Jarod told her.

"He's always doing that, but he won't tell me what he's saying," she ruffled Sam's hair. "Ready to go get some dinner?"

Sam nodded and then looked at Jarod, "Can you come with us?"

"Sam…"

Jarod ignored the warning in Melissa's voice. A sudden desire to spend some time with the young woman made him agree with Sam. Between what he'd observed himself and what Sam had said—and what the boy hadn't said—he was intrigued. "I'd love to. Is there someplace close where we can get out of the cold?"

He met Melissa's eyes and saw the hesitancy in them, but then Sam grabbed her hand and tugged on it, "Can we go to Snap Dawgs?"

Jarod raised a brow. "What is Snap Dawgs?"

Melissa grinned, and her entire countenance lit up, "Hot dogs, but not just any hot dogs. All kinds of hot dogs with all kinds of toppings and such. You won't be disappointed…unless, you're a vegetarian?"

"Not me," Jarod assured her. "I'm a red meat and potatoes kind of guy."

"Good, that's really good," she sounded relieved. "Okay, Snap Dawgs it is. How about I drive, and you can leave your truck and trailer where it is?"

Jarod nodded, "That works for me. There wasn't room for all of the trees in the lot, so we left some of them on the flatbed. My helpers already unhitched the truck and took off to find their own dinner. We'll set the rest of the trees up as room becomes available."

They headed for the parking lot. Jarod couldn't help but smile when he saw the Toyota truck Melissa was headed toward. The truck was a surprise, but the color was almost shocking. It was powder blue with a light shimmery overcoat, visible even through the layer of road dirt and the light covering of snow that blanketed the vehicle.

"Here we are," she told him with a smile. She opened the driver's door, and he watched as Sam scrambled into the back seat and buckled himself into a car seat. Jarod gave her a puzzled look, and she explained, "Colorado law requires kids under the age of eight or under seventy pounds to be restrained in a rear car seat."

"I know that, I was just wondering about the color?"

"Baby blue is my favorite. This was my gift to myself when I landed the job here in Denver. I'd never owned a truck before, but after spending one winter here, I wasn't willing to risk either Sam's or my safety in a car."

"And they just happened to have a truck painted this color?"

"Well, no. I was actually looking at a black truck, but this was a special order for someone who unexpectedly passed away before it was delivered. The dealership offered to take it back into stock and marked it down. It was better for my budget, and I really liked the color. It's a one of a kind."

"I bet it is."

"You want to know what the best thing about this truck is?" she asked. When Jarod nodded, she grinned and proclaimed, "After last month's payment, she's all mine. No more car payments."

"Congratulations. That must feel good." She nodded, and Jarod looked over his own seat, "So, Sam, tell me about this hot dog place."

Sam needed no further invitation and launched into a lengthy explanation about what was good to put on a hot dog and what was really bad. Peanut butter fell into the really bad category, while bacon and nacho cheese got a thumb's up. Jarod agreed with the peanut butter and hoped he wouldn't have to see someone consuming such a horrible combination, or he might just lose his appetite.

"I think maybe I'll stick to the normal things. Sauerkraut. Pickles. Onions. Mustard."

"Yuck!" Sam declared earning a laugh from his mother.

"Sam is a little particular about his food."

"Well, so am I. Gotta eat what tastes good. Right, Sam?"

"Right."

Jarod settled back and watched as Melissa expertly navigated what had become rush hour traffic in downtown Denver. Sam kept up a lively conversation, and Melissa expertly deflected topics she didn't want to discuss and laughingly answered others. The rapport between mother and son was very close. Yet, Jarod didn't feel like an outsider. In fact, he was already trying to figure out a way to spend more time with Melissa and her son once the festival was over, and he'd only just met them.

He began creating scenarios in his mind that would necessitate him visiting Denver on a regular basis. He also wondered what he might use to entice Melissa to bring Sam and visit his home in the mountains. There were still many months of winter left. He wondered if Melissa skied. If not, maybe he could teach her. And Sam. He was the perfect age for learning how to ski and have a ton of fun in the snow that was so prevalent in Colorado winters.

As dinner progressed, he became even more certain that he not only wanted—no, he needed—more time to get to know Melissa and her son. There was something about her that called to him in a way no other woman had ever done. He wasn't ready to put a label on it, but he most definitely wanted to explore it.

Chapter 4

A few days later…

"Melissa?" Sandy's voice called hesitantly to her from the doorway of her makeshift office. It was just before lunchtime and already, Melissa had dealt with more than a week's worth of problems.

Melissa looked up and saw the panicked look on her administrative assistant's face. "What is it?"

Sandy stepped inside the office and lowered her voice. "The mayor. He's here and asking to see the attendance numbers from the last few days."

Melissa looked through the doorway and cringed. "What is he doing here? And why is he wanting attendance numbers now? We've only been open for four nights and with the snow two days ago, a lot of people have stayed home until the weather clears."

"I don't know, but he was being rather pushy."

Melissa heard the silent plea in her friend's voice and smiled, "Don't worry about it. I'll come out and take care of whatever he needs." She grabbed her jacket, hat, and scarf and then left her desk. "Mayor Brown. To what do we owe the pleasure today?"

"Melissa. I came down to check out the festival and to see how things have been going so far."

She kept her smile in place as she automatically read between the lines. *I'm looking for a good reason to can this event and save the taxpayers some money.* She forced her thoughts back to the present, not wanting to borrow trouble if it hadn't come knocking.

"Things are going very good this year. Opening a day early seems to have helped offset the last few days where things have been a bit slower than normal. The weather is a big deterrent to people getting out at the end of the workday, but everyone seems to be responding positively to the changes we made this year. The bubble tents have allowed people to stay longer and we saw an increase of around twenty percent in the number of food vendors this year. All total, we are running a few percentage points above our attendance this many days in as we ran last year."

The mayor nodded and then pursed his lips for a moment. "Hmm. It certainly didn't look like there was a very good attendance when I arrived. The parking lot is practically empty."

"It's the middle of the workday, sir. Most people won't begin arriving until 4 o'clock or after work. You should come back this evening…"

The mayor held up a hand and stopped her with a decisive shake of his head. "Melissa, there's no good way to say this, so I'll just come right out with it."

Melissa felt her heart plummet to the ground beneath her feet, dreading whatever he was about to say.

"As you know, the city has been doing all that it can to cut expenses and make up the shortfalls in our budget these last few years. The decline in revenue from various industries has hit us hard, coupled with the number of people in the state who have been seeking financial assistance… well, the city has been operating in the red for more than two years now."

"The economy does seem to be picking up," Melissa voiced her opinion.

"Yes, but that won't cure the problem we have. The city council met in an emergency session last night, and they have voted unanimously to cancel the festival after this year."

"What?" Melissa asked, feeling as if she'd just been dumped into a large pool of water that was swirling around and around in preparation to be flushed.

"Now, I know this is a surprise, and believe me, I hate being the bearer of bad news. Your project isn't the only one being cut."

"Sir, I don't understand. The people love the festival."

"Yes, that is true, but the Museum has stepped in and offered to run a smaller version of the festival."

The Museum? How could they have possibly known to offer a solution unless someone went tattling to them and offered this up as a way to boost their bottom line. Melissa was seething mad at how underhanded this all seemed, but what could she do?

"Sir, I don't understand…how can the city pay the Museum to operate the festival and save any money?"

"The city's financial commitment to the festival will be minimal. The Museum will be charging admission to help offset the costs involved in setting the festival up."

"An entrance fee? Sir, no offense, but that has always been one of the biggest draws to this festival. Anyone can attend. People see it as a way of the city giving a little bit back this time of year."

"Melissa, times are changing. Resources are limited. I know this comes at a horrible time of year but we're not without some compassion. I want you to know that I fought for you and the city council did approve a severance package for you and your administrative assistant. Three months was all I could get. The director of the museum has also agreed to take a look at your resume, if you would like to submit it."

Melissa's mouth fell open at the audacity of this man. He'd not only been instrumental in killing her biggest project, but he thought offering her a chance to possibly apply for work with the entity taking over her project was a good thing? She started to respond out of emotion, but he turned his back on her and surveyed the festival laid out before him.

After a long moment of silence, he turned back and gave her what she and Sandy had termed his politician face. "Well, I'm sure you have plenty of things on your plate. No need to walk me out."

Melissa watched the man who had just dropped a nuclear bomb on what had been her life walk away with a little spring in his step and an off-key whistle under his breath.

I just got terminated. Sure, they're going to pay me three months out of pity or guilt, but after March next year, I no longer have a job. What am I going to do?

"Melissa, are you okay? Hon, you look like you're about to pass out." Sandy came closer, her concern etched all over her face.

Melissa looked at the young woman who had been by her side through thick and thin these last five years. She wondered how to tell her that she no longer had a job after March. She knew Sandy and her husband were saving up so that they could adopt two children from Africa but, without this job, she knew their timeframe might end up expanding from months to years. The unfairness of what had just happened had completed blindsided her. She looked at Sandy and felt tears sting her eyes.

"Melissa? What's wrong? What did the mayor want? I have the numbers he wanted, but he left without even looking at them."

"He won't be needing them now." Melissa swallowed, hating the hollow sound in her voice. She took a bracing breath and then met Sandy's eyes. "The city council met last night and voted not to fund the festival next year. The museum is going to do something with it…"

Sandy's face fell, and Melissa felt horrible for saying anything. "I'm sorry…"

"Don't be," Sandy told her. "I just can't believe they're going to get rid of the festival. And us. Right? That was why the mayor came to see you. They are getting rid of us as well, right?"

44

Melissa nodded, "I'm so sorry." Sandy stepped forward, and the two women hugged for a brief moment.

"You haven't done anything that requires an apology. And if Mayor Brown and the city council have decided to stop funding the festival, there's nothing either of us can do to stop them. Besides, it's you I'm worried about. My husband has a good paying job with benefits and a generous retirement plan."

"But, your adoption plan…"

"We have enough right now. We were trying to save up enough, so that I could take several months off right after we brought the boys home. I was planning to ask for an extended leave of absence right after the first of the year."

"You're not upset?" Melissa asked incredulously.

"I am, but I'm trying to look at the bright side here."

"There's a bright side?" Melissa asked, not seeing how losing one's livelihood right before Christmas could ever be anything but dark and gloomy.

"I won't have to worry about leaving you in a lurch when we go get the boys in April. And because the city made the decision to end our jobs, they'll have to pay me to stay home for a few months while I find something else."

Melissa mustered up a smile, "Okay, I guess I could see where that might be a good way to look at this situation. For you."

But what about me? What am I supposed to do after March?

Sandy hugged her with one arm, as they went back inside the makeshift office. "Hey, it's going to work out for you as well. This job isn't what you signed on for and has gotten way out of control. They keep pushing every year for it to be bigger and better on a smaller budget and with less manpower hours allotted for setting it up and tearing it down. I mean, just yesterday you were out there throwing snowmelt on the sidewalks because the city maintenance department said you hadn't budgeted enough for them to send someone over to handle it."

Sandy shook her head in disgust. "Face it, Melissa. They have been taking advantage of you for several years now. You could do so much more with your degree."

Melissa nodded, finding it hard to argue with her friend's observations. Things had gotten way out of control. This job had become more about manual labor some days than marketing the city. The festival had been a way to bring new people into the city during the holidays, getting them to stay overnight and spend money. It had been a huge success, or so she'd thought.

Melissa shrugged. "Maybe. I guess I need some time to process things a bit more." She felt her carefully controlled emotions waver and shook her head. "Right now, I need to head over to the tree lot and make sure Jarod gets me his invoice, so that it can be processed before Christmas. If this is the last year of the festival, then from here on out, this is going to be the best one yet."

She grabbed her purse and left the tent. She took a detour on her way to the tree lot to check on the vendors in each of the inflatable tent structures, pleased to see that everyone was set up and ready for the evening rush. She greeted each of them, many of whom had been with the festival for all five years. She debated about telling them the news, but then decided they would find out soon enough. She didn't need the added questions and worries right now. She had enough of her own to shoulder.

She headed for the tree lot, the cheerful sounds of Christmas carols wafting across the open expanse of the park. Even the sound of chipmunk voices couldn't cheer her up.

What am I going to do?

Chapter 5

"You have a wonderful Christmas," Jarod told the older couple, as he finished securing their chosen tree to the top of their vehicle. Taking a page from his parents' book, Jarod made sure every tree sold from the lot was carefully tied and wrapped in a protective green foam wrap and that the trunk was newly trimmed to better enable the tree to drink once it was inside a proper tree stand.

"Thank you, Mr. Gregory," the woman called out, as she leaned out of the passenger window. "I've always loved having a real tree but have been so disappointed when the needles fall off after only a few days."

"Well, ma'am, you follow those instructions for creating a proper tree stand, and your tree will still look good for weeks to come. Just don't forget to add water to your pot several times a day. You'd be surprised how much these cut trees can drink in a twenty-four hour period. Don't be stingy with the water either. I'd start with at least a gallon each morning and then check the water level before dinner. If it's not still at least half full, add a little more."

"We'll do it. It's the prettiest tree we've ever had," she told him, as her husband started the vehicle. She rolled the window back up.

Jarod stepped back and watched them carefully pull out of the parking area in front of the tree lot. Then, he spied Melissa making her way across the snowy field towards him. She had her head down. While she was walking with purpose, the expression on her face seemed bleak and sad. Something was definitely wrong. He had a strong urge to see if he could help fix whatever it was.

"Hey, boys. Can you hold down the fort for a while?" Jarod called out to no one in particular.

"Sure thing, Jarod," Mitch gave him a thumbs up and Jarod grinned. "Deke and I've got this."

Jarod smiled, happy that Deke had returned to the city to help out with the tree lot. Jarod had stumbled across the two high schoolers outside the church one Sunday morning the summer before. After watching them for a short time, he'd offered them part-time work out at the tree farm. They'd both been ecstatic and had never given Jarod any reason to regret his spur-of-the-moment decision. They were conscientious, hard workers, and his clients seemed to love their youthful enthusiasm and jovial personalities. Their friends had proven to be good workers as well. Jarod knew he was gaining a reputation around the county high school as the place where high school boys could get a job and earn a decent wage.

He tossed his apron aside and headed to intercept Melissa before she could trudge through the slush that lie between her present position and the tree lot. The weather had warmed up a bit yesterday afternoon. Some of the snow had started to melt, leaving nothing but dirty sludge in places that received a lot of foot traffic. The tree lot seemed to be getting more than its share of visitors and the pathway leading into the fenced lot was a muddy mess at the current time.

"Hey, Melissa. Stay right there," he hollered at her, jumping the sludge and landing in the untrodden snow on the other side. He jogged to meet her, the exercise making his blood pump and putting a big smile upon his face. "Hi."

Melissa gave him a small smile, "Hi, yourself. Were you coming to see me?"

"No. I saw you heading this way and wanted to save you having to get your boots wet."

She glanced at the ground behind him and frowned, "People shouldn't be having to walk through that mess. I'll get some of the maintenance guys to come over and lay some boards down. It's the least they can do after…"

She stopped talking, and Jarod couldn't miss the way her jaw clenched for just a minute before she pasted on a forced smile. "Never mind. I'll call maintenance just as soon as I get back to the event tent."

"Okay. You were headed to find me…because?"

She nodded and then he watched her gather her thoughts together before she looked up at him. "So, I was coming to tell you I need your invoice as soon as possible. The wheels of the machine at city hall aren't the fastest and, if I can get it submitted this week, you might actually get paid before the festival is over."

Jarod frowned and nodded, "Sure. I can get you an invoice…I was kind of waiting so that I would know how many trees sold…"

Melissa gave him a real smile then, "It doesn't matter. You did read your contract, right?"

Jarod gave her a sheepish grin, "Kind of?"

Melissa chuckled and then stamped her feet as if she were cold. "I…"

"Can we take this conversation out of the cold. Maybe someplace where we could get some food. I haven't eaten since really early this morning and I'm starving," Jarod told her.

She looked indecisive for a moment and then nodded, "Sure. How about we get out of the park for a while? There's an old-fashioned diner not far from here. I'll even drive."

"Alright. Lead the way." Jarod followed her to her vehicle, and they rode in companionable silence for most of the way, only a few comments being made about the traffic and the weather. As they pulled into the diner's parking lot, he smiled. "You weren't kidding when you said old-fashioned. How long has this place been here?"

Melissa shook her head. "I don't know. They've recently

remodeled, but they made it look like something out of the fifties. It's got a working jukebox and the requisite black and white tile on the floor. The waitresses even wear poodle skirts, minus the roller skates."

"Neat. I hope the food is good, as well. My breakfast wore off hours ago."

"You'll be pleasantly surprised," Melissa told him, walking towards the door. Jarod reached around her to hold it open, receiving a surprised thanks from her in the process. As she ducked beneath his arm, he caught a whiff of her shampoo and smiled. It was sweet, something floral but not overwhelming. It fit her personality to a tee.

"No problem. My mama raised me to be a gentleman. When her lessons didn't quite take, my daddy was right there with a quick reminder." He smiled at her as the memories surfaced. He'd had a wonderful childhood, been raised by a set of godly parents who believed it was their God-given duty to make sure he and his siblings grew up to be upstanding citizens who love God, their family and their country. Jarod was proud of his heritage, but he was also fully aware that many people didn't have the slightest idea of what a loving family was truly like.

"Sounds like you had a good childhood."

"I did. Lots of fun, work, laughter, family…it was messy at times, but that's what made it memorable. What was your childhood like?"

"It was good. My dad had a small hardware store, and my mom was a school teacher. They were older when I was born and retired shortly after I graduated from high school. They wanted to travel and, for a few years, they saw the world."

Jarod was relieved to know that Melissa had grown up in a loving family. He knew from information he'd managed to gather that she and Sam were all alone in the world now which meant she'd probably suffered the heartache of losing loved ones. When he saw a shadow cross her face, he knew he was right.

"What happened?" he asked softly.

She paused for a moment, and then took a calming breath. "My dad had a heart attack while they were camping in Alaska. I was still in college. They were deep in the wilderness and, by the time the medics arrived by helicopter, he was gone."

"Your mom was with him when he passed?"

Melissa nodded. "Yes. He was alert enough to whisper he loved her and hold her hand before he passed. She never wanted to talk about those last few minutes of his life, and I never pushed." A tear slid down her cheek. She wiped it away before sitting up straighter and taking a cleansing breath. "After he passed away, my mom just kind of seemed to give up. She didn't want to do anything or go anywhere. Sam and I moved in with her. I did my best to try to help her heal, but I think she gave up on that mountain in Alaska. She was never the same after that.

"She went downhill rapidly over the course of a few months. The doctor told me she'd given up and that her grief wasn't something anyone could cure. She died right before Sam and I moved to Denver. That was why I took this job. Sam and I both needed a change of scenery; a chance to start over where the bad memories weren't so prevalent."

"I'm sorry. That must have been so hard. On both of you." Jarod looked down and realized that he'd offered her his hand during her story, and she now clung to it like a lifeline. He squeezed it briefly and then added, "I don't mean to pry, but where was Sam's dad during this?"

Melissa shook her head. "Sam's dad left before he was even born. At the time, I was glad my own father wasn't still alive to see Tyler act to selfishly."

51

"Tyler is Sam's biological dad?"

"He provided the other half of Sam's DNA, but I don't think the term dad can be applied to him. In any fashion. My mom said I was better off starting out alone if Tyler wasn't going to step up and act like an adult. I believed her and, when he filed for divorce, I signed the papers and got rid of him."

"You were married to him before you got pregnant?" Jarod asked, disbelief in his voice.

"Yeah, he was a stellar example of a loser." Melissa told him with a wry twist of her lips.

"He doesn't see Sam?" Jarod asked, wondering how any man could call himself such and just abandon his wife and child that way.

"He didn't even want to know the sex of the baby. He asked me not to contact him and even made it part of the divorce settlement."

"Stupid!"

"Excuse me?" Melissa murmured, as the waitress came over to seat them.

"Your ex is a stupid man," Jarod told her, as he walked down the aisle behind her. They slipped into the booth and took the menus handed to them.

"I'll be back in a minute to take your order," the waitress told them, leaving as quickly as she'd seated them.

"While I have to agree with you for obvious reasons, what makes you think he's stupid?'

"He left you and then he lost the chance to get to know Sam. He's an awesome young man. You're doing a good job, mama."

Melissa blushed, "Thanks. Somedays I believe that and others...well, let's just say that I have to remind myself I'm the adult and I can't just go to my room and sulk until things get better."

A sad look crossed her face. Jarod wanted nothing more than to see a smile appear on her lips once more. "Penny for them."

She looked up and shook her head, "You'd be wasting your money."

"Let me be the one to decide that. I could tell when I saw you walking across the park that something was bothering you. More than normal, that is. You look worried a lot, you know."

Melissa shook her head and nodded. "I do tend to worry a lot, but the reason for most of that is now a moot point."

"How so?"

"The mayor paid me a visit earlier today. He and the city council have voted to end the festival after this year. He wanted to let me know now so that I could make this the best one ever. Wasn't that kind of him?" she asked, sarcasm dripping from her voice.

Melissa gave him a wry smile and then looked down and proceeded to shred the napkin she held in her hands. She hated feeling so powerless, and she didn't realize how much security this job had provided for her. And Sam. That was her main concern right now. If it was just her, she wouldn't be nearly as worried about the future. Sam deserved to have the very best she could provide for him, which meant she needed to come up with another job, and fast.

Chapter 6

"You're losing your job?" Jarod jumped right to the heart of the matter.

"Well, not right away. They expect us all to finish out the festival and then they voted to give Sandy and me three months' severance pay. Probably hoping we'd just go quietly and not cause a ruckus."

"Wow!" Jarod looked at her and then shook his head, "I don't even know what to say. Is the mayor your archenemy? I mean, he couldn't wait until after Christmas to deliver his news?"

"That's not Mayor Brown's style. He's been wanting to get rid of the festival for the last three years, and I've been going over his head and putting things in motion as soon into the New Year as I could to stay his hand. He beat me this time." Melissa shrugged her shoulders and then turned her eyes towards the table top.

"What are you going to do?" Jarod asked, his heart hurting for her.

"I really don't have a clue," she told him, the look in her eyes when she lifted her head so sad and bleak, he was surprised she wasn't crying. He watched as she mentally pulled herself up and forced a smile, "It's Christmas. I'm going to try not to think about it until January and then...I don't know. Sam and I..."

Jarod watched as her control shattered and tears filled her eyes. He reached across the table and covered her hands with his own, "Hey. It's going to be okay. This is just a little bump in the road."

Melissa shook her head, "No, you don't understand. Sam worries about me. I can see it in his eyes and when he finds out..." She pulled her hands free and wiped the tears away, sitting up a bit straighter. "I just won't tell him. Not until after the holidays are over. I can't ruin his Christmas that way. Sandy will keep it quiet if I ask her to…"

"Melissa, slow down. Sam doesn't have to know anything, but if you don't pull yourself together, he's going to figure out that something's happened. He's a smart little boy."

"I know." She gave a tearful laugh and then nodded, her expression going blank. "You're right. Okay."

"I'm sorry, I hate to interrupt, but were you two ready to order?" the waitress asked hesitantly.

"Oh. Of course. Sorry." Melissa handed her the unopened menu. "I'll have a cheeseburger, fries, and a chocolate milkshake."

Jarod listened to her order, his mouth watering and nodded. "I'll have the same but make mine a double burger with all the fixings."

"Got it," the waitress told them both, hurrying away to put the order in.

He met Melissa's eyes and could see that she'd pulled it together and was ready to move on with the rest of the day. He'd give her that, but only until he could come up with some sort of plan to help her out of her current situation. He liked fixing things. For Melissa and Sam, he'd move mountains to make sure they had something to smile about.

He handed her a fresh napkin and then smiled. "So, what were you saying about the contract?"

"The contract? Oh, your contract. You didn't read it, I'm guessing." When he shook his head, she continued, making a tsk-tsk noise in the process. "I should have checked on that before. Jarod, you aren't getting paid for how many trees you sell. They are paying you the cost of transportation and your man hours to keep the lot open. Normally, you would be paying us a rental fee for the space. We would be staffing the lot with our own personnel or volunteers. You would then give a percentage of your sales back to the city along with all of the proper fees and taxes."

She gave a rueful chuckle before continuing. "With things so topsy-turvy this year, I had them rewrite the contract, hoping to entice someone to bring some trees down here. Believe me, no one at city hall was happy with me at the time. All they could see was the loss in revenue until I reminded them that no trees meant they would also be losing revenue and taxes from the other vendors when word got out and nobody came to the festival. They changed their tune and issued me that contract I wanted. The contract you signed is actually earning you money even while you sit here with me."

Jarod looked stunned and asked for clarification. "The city is paying me to be here?"

"Yes. I need your transportation costs." She told him the mileage rate and reminded him that he needed to submit his actual fuel costs for the trip down. Everything could then be doubled to account for the trip home with any trees he hadn't sold. "You got a pretty sweet deal. How are the tree sales going?"

"We started with three hundred and sixty-five, and we've already sold over a hundred. It's only been a few days."

Melissa smiled and then sat back while their food was placed on the table before them. "Thanks. It looks amazing."

"I concur," Jarod told the waitress, as she set ketchup and mustard bottles on the table and then took her leave. "This was a great idea." He took a bite of his burger and closed his eyes in satisfaction.

"Good?" Melissa asked, watching him with a smile on her face.

He met her gaze and nodded, "Amazing."

They finished their meal, talking about non-important things, and Jarod was happy to see her smile when they finally returned to City Park. "Thanks for taking me to that diner."

"Thanks for paying for lunch. You didn't have to do that," she told him softly.

"I wanted to."

"Well, thanks again. I should probably go check to see how many new problems need solved before this evening. Sam will probably come see you once he gets out of school, unless he's becoming a pest?"

"He's always welcome. I enjoy his company," Jarod assured her. "I enjoyed your company today, as well. Let's do it again."

Melissa bit her bottom lip and then nodded, "We could do that."

"Great. Will you do me a favor?" he asked.

Melissa nodded hesitantly, as she replied, "If I can."

"Try not to think too much about the future for the rest of the festival. You deserve to enjoy the fruits of your labors."

She nodded and then her phone beeped, and she grimaced, "Time to go back to work. It seems the fruits will have to wait."

"Just don't make them wait too long."

She sighed and then Jarod watched her hurry off towards the event headquarters tent and smiled. He liked Melissa. He liked her son. What had been an obstacle in the form of her being tied to a job in Denver had just been removed, opening the door to all kinds of possibilities where Jarod was concerned.

He wanted a chance to get to know her and her son better, and a plan started to form in his mind. He headed back for the tree lot, pulling out his cell phone and making a call to the one person who would be more than willing to help him see if the feelings Melissa evoked inside of him were the kind that lasted a lifetime; his mother.

*****

Guardian Angel School

Heaven

Joy found out about the termination of the festival and Melissa's job when she arrived with Sam after school. While Sam headed off to visit the nativity and then the tree lot, Joy had hung around and listened in on a conversation Melissa and her assistant Sandy were having. She'd sensed a renewed sadness in the young mother and now she had a reason to go along with the feeling.

After checking on Sam, she decided she needed a little help with this situation. She'd been confident everything was going to work out just right, but now…she had her doubts. It seemed failure was imminent.

She arrived at the guardian angel school just as another instructional class was ending. She held back until everyone had emptied the room; everyone except the one angel she needed to see— her mentor and supervisor.

She made sure to let the door close noisily, allowing it to announce her arrival. She stood just inside the doorway until Matthias finished what he was reading and looked up at her. Only then, did she move forward while her hands twisted in front of her.

"Joy, you're looking troubled. Anything I can help you with?" Matthias asked the little angel. He'd been keeping an eye on her and her friends since he'd first learned they were having trouble with their charges.

"I don't know. I thought things were going really well, but then Sam's mom found out she's going to lose her job after the holidays. When he finds out, he's going to be really sad again with

58

worry for his mom."

"Ah. Well, let's back up for just a moment. Tell me why you thought things were going well," Matthias suggested.

Joy nodded and began listing things off. "Sam's mom and the tree guy like one another. They just need some time and then Jarod— he's the tree guy—decided to get his mom to help him. He's going to get everyone to come to Colorado for Christmas so that he can convince Sam and his mother to come to the mountains. Sam really wants a speaking part in the school Christmas pageant, but he's afraid, so I'm going to help him…"

"Joy…" Matthias said, a warning in his tone.

"Don't worry. I'm only going to give him a little dose of courage. Remind him of the things he's good at, boost his self-confidence a little bit. I won't break any of the rules."

Matthias nodded and hid a grin, "See that you don't. So far, everything you've told me sounds good."

"But his mom is losing her job. How can that be good?" Joy whined.

"Little Angel, sometimes humans find themselves stuck, afraid to move until they are forced to do so. It is in those times of forced change where they can then find the strength and motivation to make the choices that will lead them towards happiness."

"But her job…"

"…will end, and she'll make a new plan for her and Sam's future. This could work in your favor if you truly think Sam's mom and the tree guy might have a future together. He doesn't live in the city and can't move his tree farm. Maybe Sam and his mother need to consider living elsewhere?"

Silence followed his statement. He was about to reiterate his thoughts when his message finally sunk in. Joy's eyes widened, and then she started bouncing up and down in her seat.

"Yes! If Sam's mom hadn't lost her job, she would never be able to fall in love with the tree guy. Now, she can!"

Joy got up and headed for the door, only to turn around and rush back to hug Matthias, "Thank you!"

Matthias chuckled, as he watched the little angel disappear out the door and return to her earthly charge's side. He headed for the choir room, sharing a grin with Theo, the other angel charged with watching over the little guardian angels.

"Did you get her all sorted out?" Theo asked.

"Not quite, but she's learning. How are things on your end?"

"Good. I don't have any troubled angels this year. You got them all," Theo teased him.

Matthias chuckled, "I'll happily share them with you if you find yourself without anything to do." It was a common joke amongst the two instructors since last year when Theo had been the one overseeing the three little angels. Matthias had only stepped in when things with Joy had gone sideways.

"No thanks. I was in your position last year, so I'm just going to sit back and watch you deal with Joy, Hope, and Charity."

Matthias nodded, "We'll do just fine." As choir practice began, Matthias found himself smiling. He had the best job in the world—watching over the little guardian angels. He wasn't worried about them helping their charges experience the joy of Christmas. Worrying wasn't something he did.

I'll leave that to the little ones. They do it so well, needlessly, but still...they do tend to excel at worrying. Something they all need to work on.

Chapter 7

Two days later…

Melissa smiled at the elderly couple, as they left the visitor booth she'd been manning for the last hour. Sandy normally took over this task, but she and her husband had a late afternoon meeting with the attorney handling the adoption of the two African children, and she hadn't returned yet.

"Miss, could you tell me where the candle maker is located? They did come back, didn't they?"

Melissa smiled and nodded. "They're in the second tent. I believe the fourth table on your right as you enter. They have some exquisite multi-colored candles this year."

"Oh, my. I can't wait to see them. I buy two for my Christmas dinner table every year. I can't imagine how plain my table would look without them."

You're going to have to figure that out sooner than you think. Melissa nodded and then added, "You might talk to Paul and see if he has a website you could order from."

"Oh, that's a wonderful idea. We actually live in Castle Rock. Now that we're getting up there in years, coming down to Denver isn't always the most convenient thing to do. My daughters will tell you that I'm slowly embracing this new retail idea of shopping online and having the big brown trucks deliver my purchases."

Melissa chuckled, "I can't claim age, but I do some of my shopping online, too, so that I don't have to find time to fight the crowds at the local shopping mall. Merry Christmas and enjoy the rest of the festival."

In fact, I did all of my Christmas shopping online this year. Given how hectic this year's festival has been, that was a stroke of genius. Mom gets a gold star!

"Well, that's one way of soft-selling the fact that she won't be buying candles next year," Sandy said from over her shoulder.

"What am I supposed to do? Paul's one of the few vendors I've clued in and he absolutely refuses to do anything the Museum sponsors. Unless things have changed, they expect the vendors to pay for the privilege of participating and contribute a portion of their sales back to the Museum's charitable foundation."

"Isn't that kind of like double dipping?" Sandy asked with a frown.

"Most definitely. Anyway...how was your meeting with the lawyer?" Melissa asked, sliding over so that Sandy could move forward.

Sandy smiled and then spontaneously hugged her, bringing an answering smile to Melissa's face. "We're leaving April 7th to get the boys! I'm so excited I can hardly stand it."

"That's wonderful news. Your paperwork must have gone through quickly."

"The lawyer said he's never seen paperwork go through the first time without a hitch. He said the authorities usually attach a whole list of additional conditions. We were prepared to have to jump through more hoops with the African government, but that's not the case. We don't even have to stay the requisite three weeks in-country before we can take the boys on a plane and head home."

"Isn't that a bit unusual?" Melissa asked. She'd heard other friends and people at church talk about how hard some countries made foreign adoptions. She personally didn't understand why these countries wouldn't welcome Americans wanting to adopt children out of the orphanages with open arms.

"It is, but the lawyer explained that they've had so many

refugees coming in from neighboring countries. The orphanages are overcrowded and they're fearful disease will break out, and they won't have any way to stop it. There have been two more Ebola outbreaks in neighboring countries, and many people are fleeing those areas."

"That's a bit scary, isn't it?"

"A little. They have some horrible diseases besides Ebola down there. We'll have to stay in Houston for at least three weeks when we land to get the boys medical clearance to enter the country."

"Three weeks? They won't make them stay in a hospital, will they?"

"Yes, but we'll get to stay with them. It will be kind of like a small staycation. At least, that's the way we're going to handle it. I researched the hospital we'll be staying at, and they have family suites, internet, cable television, and we can bring whatever toys and such that we like. If one of the boys should test positive for something contagious, anything we bring in will have to be disposed of."

"And if the boys turn out to be perfectly healthy?"

"Then in three weeks, we can leave with everything we arrived with. Three weeks will go by fast. It will give us some dedicated time to get to know them and for them to get comfortable with us."

"Well, I'll be praying for you and the boys. I can't wait to meet them next Spring."

"I can't believe this is actually going to happen. I've been a little afraid to get my hopes up in case our adoption application was denied. Now that all of the paperwork has been signed, I've been pinching myself to make sure I'm awake and not just having a really good dream." Sandy extended her arm and pushed up the sleeve, revealing a small area by her wrist that was red from her repeated light pinches

Melissa shook her head and then warned her, "You're going to have a bruise there if you don't stop that."

Sandy gave a rueful smile and nodded. "Yeah. Okay, so enough about me. Tell me what's happening with the festival and then you can get out of here."

Melissa gave her a brief rundown and then gathered up her notes and shoved them in her briefcase. "If you're sure you're okay, I'm going to go track down Sam and head home."

"He's wandering around the festival by himself?" Sandy asked with a frown.

"Not hardly. He's with one of the high school boys helping Jarod with the Christmas trees. I think the boy's name is Mitch. Sam is absolutely starstruck by his football throwing ability." Melissa smiled and then forced the frown that wanted to form away. Sam had done nothing but talk about Mitch and Deke and how they played football, and how he wanted to play football, and asking if she knew how to throw a ball. He even asked if they could practice once the snow melted so that he'd be good enough to make the team.

It had broken her heart a little to confess to her eight-year-old son that throwing a football was not one of her talents, and that she really didn't even know all of the rules of the game. Sam had given her a sad look and then assured her he didn't need to play football. Melissa had promised to find him a mentor who did know about the game and to check into a Spring league. She'd refused to promise that league would be in the City of Denver. She needed a new job and her brief glance at the job sites only proved that she would probably need to leave Denver to find one.

She shook her head, wishing she had the same confidence and faith that her son did. Enough so that she could voice her needs to the God she knew resided in the heavens, but her faith had been shaken as of late. She wasn't sure she possessed enough to have any assurance that He would hear and answer. Sam was convinced that God needed to hear all of his childish wants, but Melissa was a bit more practical. After all, wanting and needing were too entirely different things.

Mrs. Barnes from the church would probably disagree with her. She'd told Melissa on more than one occasion that God loved to give us the desires of our hearts, but Melissa's desires seemed so trivial when compared to the massive amount of suffering present in the world. It didn't seem right for her to wish for a relationship, or a better job, or a nicer place to live, when right here in the City of Denver children went to bed hungry at night, or without knowing if any adult would be present when they woke up the next morning. God had plenty of serious matters to attend to that didn't include dealing with one single mother's occasional bouts of loneliness and depression.

"Girl, I don't know what thoughts just went through that head of yours, but you just made me lose my Christmas spirit. Stop looking so glum and go enjoy the festival you worked so hard to put together."

Melissa blinked several times and then nodded, forcing aside her dour thoughts and deciding she was going to take Sandy's advice and focus on the here and now. She couldn't do anything to change the past, and while she could possibly impact her future, she really didn't want to think about that and the uncertainties that came with it.

"Got it. I'm off to find my son, a funnel cake, and listen to some good music."

"Sounds like a plan. If you see that handsome tree man, invite him to join you. He seems to be able to bring a smile to your face."

"I don't know what you're talking about," Melissa argued.

Sandy gave her an incredulous look and waved a finger at her.

"Of course you do. Jarod is not only handsome, but exactly the type of man you and Sam need in your life. Maybe you haven't allowed yourself to think along those lines yet, but you should. It's not good for you to be alone."

Melissa stared at her friend, wondering if she'd been voicing her thoughts out loud, or if Sandy had gained the ability to read minds. Deciding it might just be coincidence, she gave her friend a nod and promised that, if she saw Jarod, she would invite him along.

It might be fun to have another adult to talk to over dinner. Sam is great, but some adult conversation would be a nice change as well.

Melissa made her way across the snow-covered lawn, veering around the nativity scene and the crowd gathered there. She could see why it seemed to draw people in, even her son. The life-sized wooden structures were one of the festival's biggest attractions, second only to the fresh cut Christmas trees that were available for purchase each year. The comments about Jarod's trees had been nothing but complimentary. She made a mental note to write him a very nice letter of reference. Hopefully, he'd be given a chance to sell his trees somewhere close next year. Maybe she'd even be in the area and able to purchase one for her and Sam's home – wherever that might be come December next year.

She headed for the tree lot, laughing as the sound of high-pitched chipmunks touted the arrival of Santa Claus. Children ran between the trees and everywhere she looked she saw couples discussing which tree they wanted to purchase. Mitch and Deke were both busy loading trees onto vehicles, and Jarod was manning the cash register. She glanced around but didn't see Sam anywhere.

She headed for Jarod, only slightly concerned that her son seemed to be missing. He saw her before she reached him and pointed to the back corner of the tent. She followed his pointing finger and then stopped as she watched her son carefully folding a stack of papers. He was concentrating with his tongue between his teeth and making sure that each fold was perfectly even and that the corners were lined up.

She paused beside Jarod and whispered, "What's he doing?"

"Folding the tree care brochures. I showed him how to do it and he promptly informed me I was in too big of a hurry and that the corners needed to match."

Melissa bit back a laugh as she asked, "He didn't."

"Afraid he did. My ego is still a bit bruised, but when he offered to take over the task, I couldn't say no."

"Sam is a stickler for details."

"A trait he no doubt gets from his mother," Jarod fired back before he turned his attention to the next customer in line. "That will be sixty-five dollars."

The man handed over the cash and then took a moment to compliment the festival. "I have to say, we didn't think last year's tree could be beat, but these trees...they are simply amazing. Give our thanks to whomever put this all together."

"That would be this beautiful lady right here," Jarod replied, grabbing Melissa's arm and turning her around so that she could accept the compliment in person. "Melissa is in charge of putting every inch of this festival together."

"Really?" the man asked. "Well, my compliments. To put together something like this so close to Christmas is simply outstanding."

"Thank you," Melissa accepted the handshake from the man. "I'm glad you're enjoying yourself."

"We are. We heard something about an ice carving contest?"

"Yes, at the end of the week. Be sure and come back for it.

Last year's contestants created some splendid pieces, and I'm sure this year will be just as awe-inspiring."

"We'll be here. Thanks again," the man nodded at both Melissa and Jarod and then headed for his vehicle where Mitch had just finished securing their chosen tree. Melissa stood there and watched the happy couple drive off a few minutes later, feeling partially responsible for this happy memory they would have forever.

"Feels good, doesn't it?" Jarod asked.

She turned her head and questioned, "What?"

"Making people happy. It feels good."

Melissa nodded. "It does. It's been the driving force behind the festival these last five years. Making people happy. Bringing them together for a few special moments in the midst of a chaotic world that demands more time and energy than a day has to offer."

"Is that what life in the city is like? Too many things to do and not enough time to even consider doing them?"

"Isn't that life everywhere?" she asked with an arched brow.

"No." Jarod didn't elaborate because Sam chose that moment to come over, the carefully folded brochures clutched in his hands. "Wow! Those look very professional. Thanks, Sam."

"No problem," Sam told him with a purse of his lips and a nod of his head. "Happy to help."

Melissa couldn't contain her laughter and asked, "What have you done with my eight year old?"

Sam handed Jarod the brochures and then threw his arms around his mother's legs. "I'm right here."

"Well, you sounded very grown up a moment ago."

"I am grown up."

"Well, a bit more grown up than you were this morning," Melissa agreed. "How about we go find a funnel cake…"

"Yay!" Sam did a little dance and then grabbed for both Melissa's and Jarod's hands. "Let's go."

"Whoa, there Sam. I have to stay here and man the cash register."

Sam's face fell and Melissa hurried to head off the tantrum she could see forming in his expressive eyes. "How about we go get the funnel cakes and bring them back here?"

"Really?" Sam cheered and then started dragging her toward the exit. "We'll be back in a few minutes, Jarod. Don't go anywhere."

Melissa tried to slow Sam down, but he was on a mission and all she could do was follow along and give Jarod a little wave. "I guess we'll be back soon."

"I'm looking forward to it," he told her softly, as she was pulled away.

So am I.

Sandy's comments echoed in her brain and Melissa found herself unable to deny the appeal Jarod held for her any longer. He was quite a man, and it seemed that she wasn't the only one who had developed feelings for him. It was clear that Sam was infatuated with Jarod, maybe even more than that. If she was honest with herself, she was heading in that same direction.

But where could such a thing go? We don't even live in the same place.

Chapter 8

One week later…

"Jarod! Jarod, where are you?" Sam's voice called out through the maze of standing Christmas trees.

"Hey, buddy. I'm right here," Jarod called to the little boy from behind him.

Sam spun around, a bright smile splitting his face as he ran up to meet him. "Guess what? Guess what?"

Jarod squatted down and smiled, "What?"

"I get to say the last line of the Christmas program!"

"Wow! That's a really important job, huh?" Jarod responded with a laugh. "Congratulations."

"Mama said I'm going to hit it out of the park." He lowered his voice and then confided, "I don't know why she was talking about hitting things when it's Christmas, but I didn't want to hurt her feelings by telling her that. You don't think Santa will hold that against her, do you?"

Jarod bit back the laughter that wanted to erupt and nodded his head, adopting a solemn expression. "First, not mentioning anything to your mom was probably a very wise thing to do. Secondly, I think Santa knows what she meant."

"Will you come watch me?" Sam asked, hope shining in his eyes.

"Sure. When is it?"

"The last day of school. Tomorrow. Will you come? Mama could bring you," Sam stated.

"Well, we should probably check that out with your mama…"

"Check what out with me?" Melissa asked, coming around an eight-foot tree with a smile on her face.

"Jarod's going to come and watch me. Can he ride with you?"

Melissa's brows went up, and she glanced at Jarod, "Did you agree to come to his school Christmas pageant or did you kind of get forced into it?'

"I would love to come watch Sam," Jarod assured her. "What time is his program?"

"2 o'clock tomorrow afternoon?" she told him hesitantly, moving a step closer as he stood up. "You don't have to come if you don't want to. I know you've been really busy."

Jarod frowned at the look in her eyes, knowing his lack of attention these last few days was to blame. After their lunch at the diner, Jarod had made an attempt to see her and Sam at least once each day, sometimes twice. They'd started eating dinner together, but then he'd been forced to spend more time at the tree lot. He'd gone several days without seeing her or Sam at all.

A few nights ago, she'd brought back a funnel cake with the intent of sharing it with him while Sam ate his own sugary confection. Jarod had wanted to do nothing more, but the tree lot had been busy right up until the time they turned the music and lights off. By that time, Melissa had already left to take Sam home and get him into bed. Jarod had apologized, but evidently his words hadn't done much to fix things. He'd missed her, and he was hoping the look in her eyes meant she'd missed him back. He just needed a few minutes alone with her to figure out where to go next.

"Hey, Mitch?"

"Yeah, boss?"

"Sam's here. Do you want to have him help you count the rest of those trees we put stands on this morning?"

"Sure thing. Hey, little man," Mitch told him, bumping Sam's knuckles lightly. "Have a good day at school?"

"Yes." Sam started talking excitedly about his role in the pageant, his little voice filling the silence of the tree lot.

"Well, that will keep both Sam and Mitch occupied for a while. I want to talk to you about something. Let's go sit inside that poor excuse for a tent," Jarod pointed to the red and green structure that sat at the side of the tree lot. It had a small heater installed inside but the warmth it offered was minimal.

"Are you complaining about the accommodations?" Melissa asked with a smile.

"Not at all, just stating the facts. If you truly want to get warm over here, you have to get inside the truck and turn the heater on full blast."

Melissa looked concerned as they stepped inside the small structure. She'd only spent time in the small canopy where the cash register was kept. "Is it really that bad..." Melissa's voice trailed off as she took in the deplorable state of the tent. "Never mind. This is ridiculous! We had problems with this same thing last year, and I know I authorized funds to purchase an entirely new tent for the tree lot. I just assumed they'd found one that looked like the outside of the old one. I'm so sorry. You should have said something sooner."

She reached for her phone, but Jarod stopped her. "Don't worry about it. There are only three days left until the festival is over. We'll survive."

Melissa left her phone in her pocket and nodded, "If you're sure..."

"I'm positive. So, I wanted to talk to you about something, and I didn't want Sam to overhear me. I want this to be your decision, and I don't want you to feel any pressure. At all."

"You're making me really nervous," she told him.

"Sorry. Look, let me back up a minute. I came up to the event tent a few days ago to see you, and I talked with Sandy."

"You talked with Sandy? About what?"

"I had just gotten off the phone with a friend back in Breckenridge. He wanted to know if I would have time to research some marketing firms here before I left the city."

"Marketing firms? For what?"

"Christmas Valley. Several of us have been toying with the idea of creating a winter escape for people to come up from the city, do a little skiing at Keystone or Breckenridge, do some shopping, take a sleigh ride, and then cut down their own Christmas tree before heading home. We want to have a Santa Village and offer the whole package."

Melissa raised a brow and shook her head. "That's a big undertaking. Something like that would take lots of planning, and lots of people..."

"It is a big undertaking. A huge one. I agree. The thing is, almost everything is already in place, we just need a way to let people know about it and to get them to drive the two hours to come and see us. We had decided to use a local marketing firm, but they've just announced that they are heading back to Texas at the first of the year."

Jarod smiled at her, "That's where I was hoping maybe you could step in. Sandy said you have a degree in marketing and designed the website for the festival here all on your own."

"I did, but you're talking about a lot of work..."

"And you're about to have a lot of time. Look, I know this is coming at you from out of the blue, so I have a proposal. Come to Christmas Valley with me for the holidays."

"What?" Melissa asked in shock.

"Bring Sam and come stay with me until after the New Year. Sam has two weeks of break coming up, and the festival will be over in just a few days. The big cabin I live in has plenty of rooms to go around. My family is all coming down from Oregon on the twenty-second. You and Sam won't have to spend the holidays alone. You'll have plenty of time to see the area and get a feel for what we want to do, and then you can give me your answer. What do you have to lose?"

Jarod could tell that he'd taken her by surprise. "I'm sorry I haven't had much time the last few days to see you and Sam. Deke had to go back to Breckenridge for a couple of days and we've been so busy, Mitch and I haven't had many breaks. Deke got back last night, so things are a little easier to manage today."

"I didn't realize you were short staffed."

"How could you?" Jarod gave her a hopeful smile and asked, "So, will you and Sam join me for the holiday?"

Melissa started shaking her head, "We couldn't…."

"What? Impose? I invited you so it's not an imposition. Look, I want you to come to Christmas Valley for more than just a potential job. I want a chance to get to know you better. These last two weeks have been…gosh, I don't even know how to explain it. I just have this feeling in my gut that tells me if I walk away three days from now, I'll regret it for the rest of my life."

He paused for a moment, watching the emotions move across her face. First surprise. Then caution. Finally, what he was hoping was a budding excitement and hope for the future. He didn't want to come off too pushy, so he asked, "Am I off-base here? Am I the only one who feels this pull between us?"

Melissa stared at him and slowly shook her head, "No, but I can't…I mean, I haven't even thought of getting involved with anyone since Sam was born."

Jarod had already assumed as much from the conversations he'd had with Sam but hearing her confirm his suspicions about how lonely her life had been made his heart hurt for her. No family to speak of, just Sam. He was a great little boy, but how much company could he really provide for a beautiful young woman like Melissa. Not enough, Jarod was sure.

"Sam's what? Seven?"

"Eight."

"And you haven't dated or gotten serious about anyone in all of those years?"

"No, I haven't had time…"

"Or you haven't made time?"

"What's the difference?"

He ignored her question and asked one of his own. "Eight years is a long time. Why not take a chance and see where this thing between us goes?"

She stared at him for so long, he began to think he might have swayed her to his way of thinking, but then he watched doubt creep into her eyes. "Jarod, I don't know how to do…" Melissa moved her hand back and forth between the space that separated them. "This."

Jarod could see the insecurity in her eyes, and he moved closer to her, leaving only a few inches between them. "Aren't you curious to find out if the attraction we feel is real?" He slowly reached out and pushed a stray strand of her hair behind her ear. "If the way your heart races when we're together means something?"

"How do you know my heart is racing?" she whispered.

"Because mine is doing the same thing." He brushed the back of his knuckles over her cheek and then leaned close to her ear and lowered his voice to a whisper. "Come home with me for Christmas. Meet my family. See where I live. Explore the opportunities that might be beyond Denver."

Melissa looked ready to capitulate and then the sound of Sam's voice calling for her reached their ears. She took a step back, shaking her head. "I can't. I have to think of Sam…I'm sorry."

Before Jarod could think to call her back, she was gone. She collected Sam and the pair immediately headed for the parking lot, with Sam arguing and turning back to look at him the entire way. Jarod watched them go, wishing there was something he could say that would put Melissa's mind at ease. He knew inviting her home with him for the holidays was a long stretch, but he was leaving Denver in three days and the thought of never seeing her or Sam again was gut-wrenching.

Needing to clear his head before he tried to deal with the public again, he headed off across the field, finding himself standing in front of the nativity scene a few moments later. He tucked his hands into his pockets and gazed down at the resin figure of the Baby Jesus.

He figured that, if Sam could express his needs to the little figure, so could he. "I know this sounds silly, but God, I need your help. There's something about Melissa that grabs my heart and it doesn't seem to want to let go. I've never felt this way before."

Jarod didn't realize he had company listening in on his heartfelt prayer until an elderly couple stepped up next to him and the gentleman patted him on the shoulder. "You just keep the faith, young fella. God hears you; me and the missus are living proof that lasting love still exists."

Just as quickly as the couple had appeared, Jarod watched them turn and wander away, holding hands and putting their heads close together as lovers are apt to do. He turned back to the nativity scene and whispered, "I have faith. I do…I just need a little direction, some help. Give me the words to say and, whatever is holding Melissa back, help me figure out how to assure her. I only want the best for her and Sam. If that's not me, well—then I'll accept that. I just want a chance to find out."

***

Joy watched Sam's mom drag him towards the parking lot and then she had observed the look on Jarod's face. He had looked so hopeful earlier, and now he just looked confused, and there was a wrinkle of worry on his brow as he wandered off toward the center of the park.

Joy had been so sure that Jarod and Melissa were meant for one another. Jarod seemed to really like Sam, and Joy had been looking forward to seeing her young charge smile more often, once Jarod and Melissa realized that they belonged together. Melissa and Sam spending Christmas in the mountains had been the perfect solution, and since Jarod had come up with the idea all on his own, Joy hadn't even skirted the guardian angel rules for meddling in human romances. Not like the year before…

She watched Melissa pull away from the parking lot and she crossed her arms over themselves and slumped down on a pile of snow, uncaring that it was stained with dirt and mud from the nearby sidewalk where it had once laid. She needed to regroup and figure out a new plan. One that would achieve her end goal and not get her in trouble with Matthias.

She heard her name called and turned to see both Hope and Charity joining her. "Hi! What are you two doing here?"

The other two angels shared a look and then Hope spoke, "We sensed that you were feeling a little lost. Is everything okay?"

"I thought so, but now…"

"Joy, you're not thinking of doing anything…illegal, are

you?" Charity asked. As the most mature of the three, she often felt the need to adopt a motherly tone.

"No! Believe me, I learned my lesson last year."

Hope put an arm around her shoulders, "We are all trying to do our very best. Have you talked to Matthias about whatever's not working?"

"Not yet."

"Maybe you should go do that instead of sitting here moping around. It's the Christmas Season and no one, especially angels, should be moping in a pile of dirty, melted ice," Charity told her.

Joy looked down, saw how dirty her gown had become and then gave Charity a sheepish look. "Guess I should probably get cleaned up before I go see Matthias, huh?"

"I would strongly suggest that," Charity informed her with a smile.

Joy stood up and then gave the other two angels a confident nod. "I will figure this out. I just need to re-work my plan."

"With Matthias' help, right?" Hope inquired.

"Of course." Joy bid the other two angels farewell and then headed off to do one last check on Sam and his mother. Seeing that they were home and that Sam was already bedded down for the night, she headed skyward to put a new plan together.

The guardian angel code came to mind, and she repeated it to herself like a mantra.

If the first plan doesn't work, go to plan B, then plan C, then plan D. Where there's a will, there is always a way. Your job is to find it.

Chapter 9

Guardian Angel School

Heaven

Joy peeked in the window of the classroom and spied Matthias standing at the window that overlooked the courtyard. She debated the wisdom of asking Matthias for clarification of a small…er, major guardian angel code; but after last year she truly didn't want to cause trouble for either he or Theo. She had come up with a new plan, she just wanted to run her idea by him and get his reaction. Her task seemed simple enough and hopefully he wouldn't shut her down before she could explain the outcome she was hoping to achieve.

She gathered up her courage, took another moment to rehearse what she was going to say, and then straightened her spine. She opened the door and then slipped quietly inside—or so she thought.

"Little Joy, what can I do for you this afternoon?" Matthias didn't even turn around to look at her.

Joy winced and walked over to face her mentor. "How did you know I was here? I was very quiet."

Matthias nodded, "Yes, you were quiet. However, I saw you enter the classroom through the reflection on the glass." He pointed to the window, and Joy grinned.

"Oh."

"Yes," Matthias agreed with an answering grin. "I also watched you standing outside the door for quite some time. Am I that scary?"

"Oh, you're not scary at all. I was simply rehearsing what I wanted to say so that it wouldn't get all jumbled and I wouldn't forget to tell you something important or explain why…"

Matthias held up a hand to halt her speech. "I get the picture. Now, you had a question or concern?"

"How did you know?" she asked.

"Little Joy, I assume you didn't stop by the classroom to talk about the weather. By the way, it's always sunny and a perfect seventy-two degrees in Heaven. So," he paused and then lowered his chin and met her eyes. "Tell me why you are here and not down taking care of your charge."

Joy nodded and then paced a bit, "So, according to the angel code we can't tamper with human emotions?"

"That is correct." Matthias's voice had grown softer now, and he was leaning forward with a crease on his brow.

"Can we tamper with situations to get a certain outcome?" she asked softly.

Matthias frowned and gave her question considerable thought before he finally answered, "I believe I would need to hear more about the situation before I could answer that."

Joy nodded and launched into a wordy and very convoluted explanation, eventually managing to convey her idea to Matthias. The short version of her plan was to create a situation where Melissa had no choice but to go someplace other than her apartment for the holidays. She intended for that place to be Christmas Valley and Jarod's farm. She just needed an unavoidable problem, or the appearance of one, to arise in the next few hours.

"Is that breaking any of the rules?" she asked him softly.

"Well, that depends. Your idea could potentially affect others besides your charge. Have you considered that?"

Joy nodded quickly. "I have. Everyone else will be

somewhere else for the holidays so the only people to be directly affected will be my charge and his mother." Joy had done her homework, making sure that her plan wouldn't negatively affect anyone other than Melissa and Sam. And Jarod, of course. He was a crucial part of her plan working.

Matthias smiled, "If you are sure no one else will be hurt, then I see no problem with your plan. Proceed and I look forward to hearing all about how it turns out."

Joy clapped her hands and her small wings spread and flapped several times. A frown from Matthias had them folding themselves in against her back.

"Sorry," she gave him a sheepish look. It was an unspoken rule that all winged angels knew; their wings were to remain unfurled when indoors for both their safety and that of the contents of the room.

Joy didn't wait for Matthias to reprimand her but nodded and muttered a quick thanks for his counsel. She skipped from the classroom, excited to put her plan into motion and knowing that she had only a small window in which to make everything work together. She spent the rest of the day setting things in motion, pleased when the other occupants of Melissa's apartment complex so readily played their part. The weather report helped move everyone's travel plans up by a day as those who were traveling through the mountains were anxious to avoid being caught in a major winter storm The exterminators also did their part, assuring the apartment supervisor that their best chance of completely eradicating the rodent problem was to have the entire building at their disposal for several days. Joy watched as things unfolded and before the sun set on that day, her plans had been completely set in motion.

She met up with Hope and Charity for choir practice and the trio compared what was happening with their charges. Joy was happy to inform her peers that she had a new plan in place and was hopeful the situation was finally under control.

"How's everything going with your charge, Charity?" Joy asked as they exited the choir room quite a while later.

"She's still immersed in grief, but she's not visiting the cemetery every day now."

"That must mean she's moving on with her life?" Hope asked.

"Slowly." Hope agreed.

"What changed?" Joy asked.

"She met someone who needed her help and it's given her something else to focus on besides how sad she is. What about you, Hope? Is your charge ready to celebrate Christmas yet?"

"No, but I'm hoping tonight will change that. She's simply forgotten the magic of Christmas."

Joy nodded and then smiled, "If anyone can remind them, it's you."

It seemed that Hope and Charity both were well on their way to handling their situations, and Joy only hoped that she would be able to say the same when she met them again on Christmas Day.

"I should probably get back to my little charge. Today is going to be the turning point and the beginning of a wonderful future."

"That's great news," Charity hugged her.

She told her friends goodbye and headed back down to earth to where Sam and Melissa were preparing for the start of another day. And what a day it was going to be!

***

Melissa yawned and then shook her head and forced herself to crawl out of bed and make her way to the shower. She went through the motions of getting ready for her day, keeping one eye on the clocks scattered throughout the apartment the entire time. When the clock reached seven o'clock, she put a smile on her face and tapped on Sam's bedroom door as she waltzed through it and pulled the curtains open.

"Rise and shine, sleepyhead. Today's your big day."

Sam squirmed beneath the covers. She started to reach for the bottom of the blanket, already anticipating the struggle she was going to have getting him up and ready for school. Just as she wrapped her fingers around the blanket, he insisted on sleeping with, his head and shoulders popped out from under the other end.

"Mom! Today's the Christmas pageant!"

Melissa smiled and released the blanket. "I know. Are you excited? Just a little bit?" she held her fingers just a half an inch apart.

Sam threw his arms wide and replied, "I'm excited this much!"

Melissa chuckled and then headed for the hallway. "Get dressed, wash your face, comb your hair, and then meet me in the kitchen for breakfast."

"Got it."

To her surprise, he was already out of bed and digging through his dresser drawers before she'd taken half a dozen steps. Deciding to accept the easy morning she was having, she quickly started the coffee pot and popped some bread into the toaster. Melissa was running a bit sluggish this morning, mostly because of her last exchange with Jarod the night before. She knew she'd acted immaturely by taking Sam and leaving the way she had. Now, she needed to figure out how to handle the situation when she saw him next. At a minimum, she felt like she owed him an apology, and he deserved an explanation. If only she had a valid one.

The toaster popped up, and she glanced down the hallway once more. After listening for a moment and not hearing the sound of little feet coming down the hallway, she called out, "Sam, you're going to be late for school if you don't come eat your breakfast right now."

She pushed aside the tiredness that was pulling at her from staying awake late into the night, thinking about the questions Jarod had asked her.

"Don't you want to see where these feelings can take us?"

She still couldn't believe he'd invited her and Sam to come home with him for Christmas. The idea was ludicrous when she tried to think about it logically, but then her heart got involved and reminded her how long it had been since she'd let anyone besides Sam into her life. Doubts had kept her awake for hours. She only wished she'd had someone to talk to about it. As always, she was alone. The only person she'd had to confide in since moving to Denver was Sandy. Melissa had refused to call her assistant and friend at three o'clock in the morning just to complain about the possibility of having a relationship.

I'm not even making much sense now. Maybe I should relax and just let things unfold naturally and stop trying to analyze everything.

"Sam!" she called once more.

"I'm coming," Sam hollered back, running into the kitchen and then sliding to a stop next to the table in his stockinged feet. "Oops! I forgot my boots."

"You can put them on in the car. Sit down and eat," Melissa

tousled his hair a bit and then smiled when he sat on the edge of the chair and began shoveling multi-colored cereal into his mouth. She buttered both pieces of toast, applied a generous coating of peanut butter, and then handed one to Sam and kept one for herself.

When he picked up the toast and tried to take a bite with his mouth still full of cereal, she made a tsk-tsk sound and advised him, "Slowly. Chew your food or you'll get a tummy ache."

She finished packing his snack and then tucked it into his backpack.

"Not today," Sam told her with a negative shake of his head. "Today's going to be an awesome day!"

Melissa smiled down at her son, "And why is that?"

"Because...mom! You know. You told me when you woke me up."

"That's right. I did, didn't I? I wasn't sure you were actually awake. Refresh my memory."

"It's the Christmas pageant, and you and Jarod are both going to be there."

Melissa held her smile in place; the conversation she'd had with Jarod from the day before replaying in her mind. She had finally gotten honest with herself in the wee hours of the morning and admitted that she'd like nothing more than to take him up on his offer to join him and his family for Christmas, but fear held her back.

Her ex leaving her when he found out she was pregnant had been overshadowed by her excitement at being pregnant. She hadn't really allowed herself the time to feel hurt over his loss and had just assumed she'd gotten over it. She'd been wrong. Tyler's abandonment had left her wary of relationships, so she'd gotten very good at avoiding them altogether. Until now. Until Jarod had walked into her life.

Melissa glanced at her watch and pulled her mind back to the present. "Buddy, we have to go. Now."

"I'm ready," Sam pushed away from the table, lunging for his backpack and his boots at the same time. "Race you to the car."

Melissa smiled, grabbed her day bag and followed her son to the front door. Sam was still standing there when she reached him. He turned and thrust a piece of paper into her hands. She glanced at it and then him.

"What's this?'

"I dunno. It was taped to the door. I'm gonna win," Sam told her, the competition still on in his mind.

Melissa nodded and stepped out of the apartment, her eyes skimming the paper at the same time. She stopped with her hand on the doorknob and shook her head as she re-read the notice.

"They can't do this!"

Sam heard her and hollered from the backseat, "What can't they do?"

Melissa glanced up and then shook her head, her protective instincts kicking in. "Nothing. Hey, let's get you to school."

Sam beamed, "I won."

"Yes. You won."

And this piece of paper may have just ruined Christmas! First, I lose my job. Not right away but knowing three months into the New Year I'll be jobless is kind of hard to ignore. Now, I can't even be at home for Christmas with my son. This has got to be the worst Christmas on record.

Chapter 10

Melissa's mood continued in a downward spiral after she dropped Sam off and headed for City Park. She'd gotten three text messages from city workers about a problem with some of the electrical that had been set up to accommodate the festival. They were getting replacement generators on the way but, in the meantime, some adjustments needed to be made.

With only three days of the festival left, she just wanted everything to go smoothly. For once! In five years, she'd never had a problem come up that she couldn't deal with. The Christmas trees had come closest and, by some miracle, Jarod had arrived, and her problem had gone away. Electrical issues weren't anything new. She was suddenly so tired of having to deal with problems. As the streetlight turned red, she decided to tackle that particular problem head on.

She used the Bluetooth in her truck and called the city maintenance department on her drive from the school to the park. The light turned green just as the call connected.

"Maintenance," a cheery voice answered the call.

"Jenna? This is Melissa. Where's Jim?"

"Uh, hey Melissa. Jim's not here, but he told me you'd be calling, and he wanted you to know that he's on top of things and was headed over to City Park to speed things along."

Melissa blew out her breath, as she braked to a stop at another red light. "Is that supposed to make me feel better or worry me more?"

Jenna chuckled, "This time of year, I can't even hazard a guess. He was mumbling something about bubble enclosures? Does that help?"

Melissa groaned, "No, not at all, actually. Have you been over to the festival yet?"

"No. My fiancé and I are going tonight to pick out a tree."

"Well, we brought in these bubble tents to help provide some added protection from the unpredictable Denver weather and the cold. They are kept inflated by warm air that is…"

"…put out by the generators," Jenna finished for her with a groan of her own. "No wonder he was in such a poor mood. Look, I'll keep you updated…"

"No need. I'm almost to the park now. I have a few things to take care of and then I'll wander in that direction and hope that they have everything fixed by then."

God, if you're up there listening, a little help right now would be appreciated. I don't even want to imagine the chaos that will ensue if one of those bubbles collapses.

"Okay. Try to have a better day?" Jenna suggested.

Not gonna happen, she thought as she glanced at the notice lying on the passenger seat. "I'll try," she murmured automatically, before disconnecting the call and finishing her morning commute.

She parked and marched towards her makeshift office, giving Sandy a tight smile. Sandy immediately sensed her mood and followed her.

"What's wrong?"

Melissa handed her the notice at the same time she pulled out her cell phone and dialed the superintendent for her apartment building.

"That is what's wrong."

Sandy read the notice and her brows disappeared into her hairline. "Wow! Talk about bad timing."

"Yeah," Melissa agreed sarcastically. "What I want to know

is if they can even do what that letter says is going to happen."

"I don't know, but they probably can. What are your neighbors going to do?"

"I don't know and frankly, I can't be worried about them. I assume most of them will be visiting family over the holidays like in the previous years. All but two of them are college kids from out of state. Normally, Sam and I are the only ones in our building until after New Year's."

A gruff voice answered the phone and Melissa wasted no time in getting to the point, "Mr. Alexander, this is Melissa…."

"Oh, hey! Melissa," the man's voice brightened. Melissa had a mental image of the man with greasy hair and his shirt always unbuttoned halfway down his chest, grinning smarmily into the phone. Oliver Alexander thought he was a gift to every woman he met. Melissa had yet to meet anyone besides the man's doting mother who actually held that belief. "It's great to hear your voice."

Melissa tried not to let her temper explode, "I wish I could say the same. I'm calling about the notice you left on my front door?"

"Oh, yeah. Sorry about that but the exterminators need the building empty for several days while they get rid of the little vermin."

"I haven't seen any evidence of mice in my apartment…"

"You're lucky then. They did an inspection yesterday and found several large nests of the critters in the basement and in the apartment next to you. They've eaten through the insulation between the floors and the last thing I need is for them to get stuck in the walls and die. That's why we need the entire building empty. The contractors are going to seal up all of the holes they can find, and the exterminators are going to trap and remove all of the mice in the building before this problem goes any further."

"Mr. Alexander, you do realize you're asking us to leave during Christmas?"

"Hey, call me Oliver."

"Mr. Alexander…," Melissa closed her eyes for a brief moment as she attempted to hold onto her composure. Screaming at the man in frustration wouldn't accomplish anything. "Couldn't the exterminators deal with the mice in everyone else's apartment? You're asking me to leave my home. The one I pay you very well for every month."

"Well, yes, but everyone else told me they were going to be gone…and it's just for a few days…I just assumed…you were planning to go someplace else, right?"

"Wrong. Sam and I were planning to stay at home this Christmas." *Just like we always do.*

"Er…well, that won't be possible now." Mr. Alexander paused and then lowered his voice, "You and Sam could always come stay with me…"

Melissa shook her head, pushing back the shiver of revulsion that crawled up her spine.

Not if yours was the last standing building in the entire city.

Mr. Oliver Alexander was the stereotypical dirty old man, only he wasn't all that old and he took being dirty to a whole new level. He'd been putting the moves on her since the day she'd looked at the apartment and agreed to move in. He'd invited her out to eat numerous times. She'd turned him down each and every one of them. Melissa had done her best to avoid interacting with the man. He just didn't seem the type to take rejection lightly.

She cleared her throat. "No! I mean, thank you for the offer, but we'll make other arrangements. When do we need to be out?"

"Two days from now? The exterminators will be there first thing in the morning three days from now."

Great! The last day of the festival. "Fine. Goodbye."

"Melissa wait…"

She hung up the phone without waiting to hear whatever the man was going to say. She took a deep breath and looked up to see Sandy watching her carefully. "Everyone else is going to be out of town. We have to be out the last day of the festival and, according to that notice, we won't be allowed back into the building for at least a week."

Sandy stepped forward, "You and Sam will come home with me then. We'd love to have you with us for Christmas."

"Sam and I couldn't impose on you that way. Besides, don't you have all kinds of family coming to visit?"

"Sure, but we can put sleeping bags on the floor…"

"No way! I'm not putting your family on the floor." Melissa wouldn't intrude on Sandy's family gathering. Especially with everything going on between losing their jobs and the adoption finally being approved. Sandy deserved to have a wonderful Christmas, and Melissa and Sam weren't going to be third wheels.

"Well, what are you going to do then? Spend Christmas in a hotel?"

"If I have to." Melissa's phone vibrated, and she grimaced. "Before I deal with my living arrangements, I need to go see what's happening on the other side of the park. Something about the electrical being down."

Sandy gave her a sympathetic smile, "It's always something around here."

"I'll be back as quickly as I can." Melissa pulled her gloves back on and headed for the side exit. She'd deal with the electrical problem and then go to Sam's play. Maybe somewhere in between the two, she could figure out where she and Sam were going to be spending Christmas this year.

Chapter 11

Several hours later…

"Good afternoon, Sandy," Jarod called out to Melissa's second-in-command. "Where's the boss lady?"

Sandy gave him a shake of her head, "I wish I knew. With the way today has been going, I wouldn't blame her if she ran away and joined the circus."

Jarod frowned, "I didn't know the circus was in town."

"Well, it might not be one with elephants and tigers, but believe me, she's been dealing with a circus all day long. The electrical has been giving the city workers fits in the park today, someone slid into the security shack in the parking lot…"

"Was everyone okay?" Jarod asked concerned.

"Everyone was fine. It happened early this morning before anyone got here. And if that wasn't enough, she called more than a dozen hotels and not a one of them had any vacancies."

"Hotels? Why is she calling hotels?" Jarod asked.

Sandy sighed, "Her apartment is being fumigated and repaired in a few days. She got the notice this morning that she has to vacate the premises for at least a week."

Jarod was puzzled and tried not to let his feelings get hurt that she'd been calling hotels instead of just taking him up on his offer.

Maybe she doesn't think it's still on the table since she already declined?

Testing the waters, he asked, "Did she happen to mention my conversation with her the other day?"

Sandy shook her head, "No. What conversation?"

Jarod quickly explained about the marketing need for Christmas Valley, ending with his invitation for her to join him for the holidays. "She said she had to think about Sam."

Sandy nodded her head. "That sounds like Melissa. She always puts that little boy first. I'm not surprised she turned you down. Personally, I think you two make a cute couple and the chemistry between you seems promising...that's probably not working in your favor. She probably wouldn't admit it, but her ex dumping her had to have left a mark."

"You think she's scared?" Jarod hazarded a guess.

"I'm thinking it might be more like terrified that she might actually let herself feel something for you and risk getting her heart broken again. Only, this time it would involve Sam's heart as well. That's going to be a hard battle to win."

"So, any suggestions?" Jarod asked.

Sandy nodded and then grinned. "Use your charm."

Jarod nodded back and glanced at his watch. "Okay, now I really do need to find her. Sam's Christmas pageant starts in an hour."

Sandy reached for her radio. "Melissa, are you out there?"

Static crackled and then her voice filled the small space. "I'm over by the parking lot. What's up?"

"Jarod is here looking for you. Something about Sam's..."

"...Christmas pageant. Tell him to meet me at the truck, and we'll go from there. Otherwise, we're going to be late."

"I'm on my way," Jarod told her. "Thanks, Sandy."

"No problem. Good luck. For what it's worth, I hope she and Sam spend the holidays with you, and she's able to find a place where she can truly be happy. Denver isn't it."

Jarod nodded and left, heading for the parking lot. He saw her before he got there and decided to wait until after the pageant to let her know that he was aware of the notice she had gotten this morning. He wasn't sure how the conversation would go, but he was hoping that, before the end of the day, she would agree to join him for the holidays in Christmas Valley.

***

Two hours later…

"Merry Christmas to all and to all"—Sam paused dramatically and executed a deep bow, then stood and flung his arms out—"a Good Night." He beamed as the audience burst into applause.

"He did an excellent job," Jarod murmured in Melissa's ear.

Melissa nodded. "He did. Look at him, he's so proud of himself."

The parents and other spectators stood to their feet, applauding the students for a Christmas pageant to remember. The teacher said a few words, wished everyone a marvelous Christmas break and then dismissed the children to go find their parents.

Sam wasted no time and ran right up to them.

"Did you hear me?" he asked, hugging his mother first and then flinging himself against Jarod's legs.

"We did, Sam. You did a very nice job," Jarod told him, brushing a hand over his hair.

"You were fantastic," Melissa told her son.

Sam's response was to wrap both arms tighter around his legs. Jarod squatted down and hugged him close, his heart melting a bit when Sam eagerly hugged him back. When he looked up, he

94

couldn't quite interpret Melissa's expression.

"Thanks for coming," Sam told Jarod a moment later.

"No problem. Thanks for inviting me."

"Hey, Sam! Let's go get some cookies," another child called from a few feet away.

Sam looked at his mother. "Can I?"

Melissa nodded. "Sure. Go ahead."

Jarod stepped closer to her, as they both watched him scamper off with his friends. Sensing a nervousness in her, he asked quietly, "Want to tell me what that look was all about?"

Melissa met his eyes and then shook her head, dropping her gaze. "Not really. Let's just say it's been a really long day."

"I get that," Jarod told her. "How about I take you and Sam for an early dinner? I need to be at the tree lot tonight, but not until 5:30."

"The ice carving competition begins tonight, so my day is only half over right now. If the city guys can't get the lighting situation fixed, they may be carving by moonlight."

"I'm sure they're getting it all figured out," he assured her.

"I hope so. I should get Sam, so that we can go. I've got so many things to do still…"

"Anything that can't wait for an hour or so?" Jarod asked as they began making their way across the school auditorium to the cafeteria doors where the snacks were laid out on decorated tables.

"I guess not."

"Good." They found Sam, and Jarod waved him over. "How about we go get some dinner?"

Sam looked at his friends and then asked, "Pizza?"

Jarod shrugged and looked at Melissa, "Is that okay with you?"

Melissa nodded but she had a strange look on her face that turned to full on mirth when Sam spoke up again. "I wanna go play."

Jarod got the impression that he was missing something, but he asked anyway, "Play?"

Melissa licked her bottom lip and explained, "He wants to go to *Chuck E. Cheese's*."

"Ah. My nieces and nephews like that place as well. They're all within a few years of his age." Jarod paused for a moment, telling himself he could grab something more substantial to eat at the festival. The children's pizza place was known for a large dancing mouse and lots of arcade style games, but in his experience, only a child would think their pizza was edible.

Seeing Sam watching him with hope in his eyes, Jarod nodded, "That works for me, and it will give us a chance to talk."

"Talk?" Melissa asked, nervousness back in her eyes.

Jarod decided to ignore her question and placed a hand on Sam's shoulder. "You up for helping me with trees tonight?"

Sam nodded, reaching for both of their hands. He swung lightly between them, chatting away about everything that had happened that day. He kept up the talk as they drove across town and then waited to be seated at the children's playground that also masqueraded as a pizza parlor. Sam wasted no time in taking the coins that came with their pizza and heading for the skeet ball tracks.

Jarod watched him for a minute and then turned back to Melissa, "Is he any good?"

"You'll see. So, you never answered my question. What did you want to talk about?"

Jarod faced her fully and searched her eyes for a long

96

moment. "You've had quite a day. I talked with Sandy earlier. She told me about your apartment."

Melissa shook her head, and her face closed down. "She had no business telling you that."

"I think she didn't realize she'd done so until it was too late, but why wouldn't you tell me yourself. She said you were having trouble finding a hotel, but I've already invited you and Sam to spend the holidays with me."

"I didn't think that offer was still open," she murmured, her eyes cast downward on the table, as she worried the napkin in front of her. "I turned you down."

"Yes. You did." Jarod reached across the table and covered her hands with his own. "Melissa. Look at me. Please?"

She swallowed audibly and then lifted her head. He searched her eyes and addressed the fear he saw lurking there. "I know you're scared of getting hurt again. I don't want either of us to get hurt, most especially not Sam. Come up to the mountains with me. It will give you a place to celebrate Christmas with Sam and give us an opportunity away from the stress of the festival to see where this leads."

"Jarod, I really want to say yes. I was up late thinking about things, and I realized I never really dealt with my ex leaving me. I found myself getting mad and feeling hurt early this morning. I hated the way those two things made me feel."

"Natural emotions to feel."

Melissa shrugged her shoulders and gave a short nod. "At the time, I had a baby to look forward to. I guess I just pushed how I felt about Tyler's actions to the back of my mind and never dealt with them. Now…I'm afraid that I wouldn't have any way to cope if I was to get let down again."

97

"Why are you so sure that I would let you down?" Jarod asked.

"I'm not." She paused for a long moment and then softly told him, "Jarod, I told you yesterday that I don't know how to do this. I haven't even been on a date since before I got married."

Jarod smiled and picked up one of her hands, brushing his thumb across her knuckles. "No pressure and no need to worry or fret. Just be yourself. Be honest with me and we'll see where this goes. As far as dating goes, we've already been on several dates, but you weren't nervous because we didn't label them. So, don't label what's happening between us at all."

Sam chose that moment to come back to the table, his hands filled with tickets which he'd won by playing skeet ball. "Jarod! Mom! See how many tickets I got?"

"Wow! You must be pretty good at that game, huh?" Jarod asked, giving Melissa a moment to compose herself even as he released her hands. He saw Sam's eyes watching their clasped hands and couldn't miss the smile that grew on the little boy's face. "How about we leave your tickets with your mom and go wash our hands before the pizza gets here?"

Sam looked at him and then eagerly nodded. "Sure. Here, mom. Watch these, okay. Jarod and I are going to the men's room."

Jarod looked at Melissa and was pleased to see that her face had cleared. He leaned down and asked, "Is going to the men's room a treat?"

Melissa nodded and whispered back, "I normally make him use the ladies' room or the family restroom. I don't like the thought of him being vulnerable inside the men's room where I can't go."

"Got it." He straightened and waved a hand in front of him, "Lead the way, sir."

Sam giggled, but instead of bouncing ahead, he grabbed Jarod's hand and started swinging their arms back and forth. Jarod squeezed his little hand back. As they headed for the corner of the building, he glanced back at Melissa who was watching them interact.

She'd let her guard down a little bit; he could see the longing in her eyes. She wanted what he was suggesting. That gave him hope that these feelings growing inside of him weren't in vain.

As he waited for Sam to finish playing in the foamy soap a few minutes later, he looked at their reflection in the mirror. He wanted to be the man in the mirror with the little boy as he grew into a teenager and then a man. He wanted to be the one standing beside Sam's mom years from now when he finally left the nest and forged his own path in the world. He just needed a chance to convince her that they belonged together. And maybe a little help from the Man upstairs.

Chapter 12

The next evening…

"And the winner of this year's ice carving contest goes to Randy and Sherilee Andrews," Melissa spoke into the microphone. She smiled as the group gathered around them clapped while the brother and sister team came forward to accept their award.

Melissa handed them the trophy. "Congratulations, you two. What does this make? Two or three years now?"

"Three," Sherilee answered in her quiet voice.

"Well, congratulations. A job well done." Melissa watched them scamper away to receive their friends and family's accolades. She switched the microphone off and turned to set it down, only to find herself with her nose buried in Jarod's down jacket. "Oomph!"

"Whoa! Didn't mean to startle you. Are you okay?"

Melissa straightened herself and nodded, "I'm fine. What are you doing over here? I thought you had to help manage the tree lot tonight?"

"I do," Jarod told her with an easy smile. "I came over to see if you wanted to come hang out at the tree lot with Sam and me for a bit?"

Melissa nodded. "Sure. The festival ends for the night in another hour, anyway. Thanks for letting him hang out with you. Again."

"No problem. He's a great kid. I've really enjoyed having him around. Only one more day to go and the festival will be over for another year."

"You mean for the last year and last time, don't you?" she asked him, not bothering to keep the sour note from her voice.

"Yes, but I've learned that, when God closes one door, there's usually another one already starting to open. The festival is just a door closing."

"A great analogy, but that doesn't make the uncertainty of the future feel any less stressful," she told him.

"Yeah, I know. Talk is cheap in situations like this. Come on, let's go get your mind off of the future."

Melissa nodded and forced a smile. "I don't think that's possible, but I'm willing to try."

Jarod smiled and then waved her onto the path before him. He joined her, reaching out and capturing one of her gloved hands in his own. She glanced up at him, but she didn't pull her hand away. Walking this close to him felt so natural. Yet, it was something she hadn't done in so many years, she found herself having trouble processing how she truly felt about it.

On the one hand, Jarod seemed to embody everything she'd always admired about the perfect man who, one day, might become her husband and the father to her children. Tyler had obliterated her ideal future and, until the last few weeks, she'd begun to think her dream was gone, never to be resurrected again. It seemed maybe she was wrong.

He squeezed her hand. She glanced up to find him watching her carefully. "You look like you're trying to figure out some great problem. What happened to putting thoughts of the future aside for a while?"

Melissa bit her bottom lip and nodded. "I...I failed?"

Jarod squeezed her hand again. "Try harder. But first, tell me what's put that frown between your eyes?"

Melissa took a breath and then spoke her mind—or the part she was able to put into actual words. "This...whatever is happening between us is confusing."

Jarod pulled her to a stop. "Why is it confusing? I like you. I think you like me."

Melissa made a face and shook her head, "You make it sound so easy."

Jarod turned her to face him, his hands remaining on her shoulders as he took a small step closer to her. "This should be easy. And exciting. And not something you fear or run away from."

He searched her eyes and Melissa held his gaze, seeing something in his eyes that sparked a warmth inside her chest that she hadn't ever felt before. Ever. Melissa felt butterflies take flight in her stomach, as he stepped closer. She could see the tiny lines at the corner of his eyes.

"Melissa, please take a chance on me. On us. I know it's scary...I'm scared too. If I've learned anything in this life, it's that you have to take chances or live with regrets. You've had a night and most of today to think about things. Come home with me for the holidays."

Melissa bit her bottom lip. "I should say no." But her heart really wanted her to say yes. She heard Sam's laughter and turned her head to see him talking with several shoppers. She realized he was growing up right before her eyes. Sam had taken to Jarod. She had to fight back tears when thinking that his own father would never see what a marvelous young man he was becoming.

"Melissa?" Jarod's hand smoothed her hair back. She looked back at him, deciding in a moment's time to take that leap of faith and give whatever was happening between them a chance. For Sam's sake. And for hers.

She nodded. "Yes."

Jarod's brow rose. "Yes? You'll come home with me for

Christmas?"

Melissa nodded, biting her bottom lip as a smile tried to burst forth. "Yes."

Now that she'd made her decision, she felt like a soda pop that someone had shaken up and then taken the top off. Excitement was blossoming inside her. It seemed to be echoed by Jarod who was smiling broadly at her. Melissa smiled in return just as her son's body slammed against her from behind, pushing her into Jarod.

Oomph!

Jarod wrapped his arms around her instinctively. Gazing up at him, she felt the breath freeze in her lungs.

"Mommy! Mommy! I sold a tree, all by myself!" Sam seemed oblivious to the fact that he'd just crashed into his mother and thrown her straight into Jarod's arms.

Melissa brought her hands up and pushed herself out of his arms. He reluctantly let her go.

"That's wonderful, Sam. Really."

"Hey, buddy. Great job," Jarod stepped around her and gave Sam a high five, providing Melissa the precious moments she needed to get her riotous feelings under control once more.

She cleared her throat and then bent down and hugged Sam, "I'm proud of you."

"Thanks! Jarod, can I help you sell trees tomorrow, too?" Sam asked, hopping from foot to foot.

"Easy there, buddy. I don't mind, but you'd better ask your mom. Tomorrow's the last day of the festival, and she might need your help elsewhere."

"Mom?" Sam turned imploring eyes towards her. "Please?"

Melissa chuckled, "Of course you can. You only have half a

day of school tomorrow."

"Yes!" Sam pumped his fist into the air.

Melissa and Jarod chuckled and then she waved her hand to get his attention. "I have some more news I think you might like."

"What is it?" Sam asked, coming to a halt in front of her.

"Well, remember that letter you found on the front door?" When he nodded, she continued, "It was a letter telling us that we would need to find someplace else to sleep for a few days while they fumigate for mice."

Sam frowned. "We don't have mice."

"No, but other people in the apartment might have complained. Anyway, Jarod thought maybe we would like to spend Christmas with him in the mountains."

Sam paused for a moment, and Melissa worried that maybe she'd overestimated how much he seemed to like Jarod. But Sam's brain finally caught up. He looked between the two of them, joy spreading across his face, as he began dancing around and making enough noise to awaken the entire zoo two blocks away.

"Sam! Hey buddy, quieten down before you wake up everything for miles around."

Sam made an effort to stop his mad dance of jubilation, and lower his voice, but it seemed to be taking all of his self-control. Jarod placed a calming hand on his shoulder, "I take it you won't mind spending Christmas at my place?"

"No! This is awesome!" He flung his arms around Jarod legs, and then did the same with Melissa, once more almost causing her to tumble over. Jarod was there with a supportive hand and a word of caution.

"Whoa there, Sam. Don't knock your mom over."

"I won't. Do we really get to go home with Jarod?" he asked, his eyes alight with hope and a joy that Melissa had never seen before. She nodded, and he flung himself against her legs again. When he released her, he did a little victory dance, complete with a weak imitation of an Indian war cry.

"I take it he's happy?" Jarod asked with a smirk and a chuckle.

Melissa nodded, "Very." She paused and then allowed a smile to break across her face, "So am I. Scared, but excited, if that makes any sense."

Jarod wrapped an arm around her shoulders while they watched Sam continue to celebrate by dancing. "It makes perfect sense. This is going to be the best Christmas ever."

***

Guardian Angel School

Joy was so happy. She returned to the guardian angel school and executed several full somersaults in the air as she made her way to the classroom. She found Matthias sitting inside, watching her with an indulgent smile upon his angelic face.

"Joy, can I assume the happiness you're exhibiting is due in part to a new development with your young charge?"

"Yes! It's wonderful news. It's a beautiful time of the year," she announced with a little twirl.

Matthias chuckled. "That it is."

"Sam is so happy! His mother took a leap of faith; they are going to the mountains to celebrate Christmas with the tree man. I can tell they like each other. Sam is so happy."

Matthias looked at her solemnly for a moment and then

105

asked, "How many rules did you break?"

Joy laughed and executed another pirouette. "None! Melissa and Jarod really do like each other. They may be falling in love."

"I'm glad things are working out, but remember; you cannot influence human emotions," Matthias warned her.

Joy nodded her head. "I know. I won't."

She made the angel promise sign and then danced her way back out of the classroom. She was going to join the angel festivities for a little while and then she'd pop back down and see how Sam and his mother were doing. She couldn't wait till the annual guardian angel get together right after Christmas. She was confidant she would be sharing a happy outcome for her young charge and couldn't wait to hear how her other angel friends were doing with their challenges.

Chapter 13

Approximately twenty-four hours later…

"Mom! Come on. Jarod is ready to go," Sam called into the almost empty tent that had been Melissa's office in City Park for the last several weeks.

It was nearing ten o'clock at night. The festival had ended over an hour earlier. For good. This was the last time she'd spend the weeks leading up to Christmas solving problems at City Park and using a tent as her temporary office. She looked at the now cleared table she'd been using as a workspace and felt a wave of sadness sweep through her.

Changes were coming and neither she nor her vendors were happy about it. In fact, the only person happy about cancelling the festival was Mayor Brown. He hadn't gotten her vote the first time around. That wouldn't be changing when he came up for re-election. He kept saying the changes were necessary to balance the city's budget, but Melissa knew firsthand how much waste went on at the highest levels of government. If they wanted to cut expenses, she'd be happy to give them a list of programs and positions that were a complete waste of taxpayer money.

"Mom!" Sam called again, impatience growing in his voice.

Sighing, she took one last look around the tent and dropped the files she was holding in the half-empty box that was waiting to be hauled back to the physical office space. She didn't have to worry about that part of the festival as the heavy lifting would fall to others. Tight shoulders had her silently thanking the powers that be for their suggestion years ago about allowing the maintenance department to handle its tear-down. It was a suggestion she'd taken and never regretted once.

The city workers would take care of the cleanup; removing the trash, melting ice sculptures, stage, and other structures that had been erected just for the festival. They had headed home for the evening, though, leaving the cleanup until the light of day. Everyone was tired and ready to head to their respective homes for a good night's sleep. Including Melissa.

She covered up a yawn, realizing it was growing very late and her day wasn't quite over yet. Unlike the other city workers who were enjoying the comfort of their own homes this evening, she and Sam couldn't go back to her tidy little apartment. At least, not for the next week. Instead, they were going to travel to Jarod's home and spend Christmas with him and his visiting family. Melissa had been nervous all day. Now that the moment to leave was at hand, she felt almost sick with worry and *what ifs*.

What if his parents didn't like her? What if she and Jarod really didn't have that much in common and, after spending a single day together, they couldn't stand being in the same room with one another? She and Sam would be stuck in a place with people they didn't know for the next week.

"You all ready?" Sandy asked, coming back into the tent for one last look around.

Melissa shoved her worries aside and nodded. "I think so. I packed the last of the contracts and such in one of the boxes earmarked for the office."

She picked up the last stack of files, maps of the festival, and vendor contracts and hugged them to her chest for a moment. Everything was packed away, just this last pile of folders remained.

"I'll take care of putting them away when I come back from vacation. I can't believe we actually have the next little while off."

"You mean the next long while?" Melissa corrected her, a sour note coloring her voice.

"Hey! It's Christmas. The festival was a success, and you have two handsome men waiting outside for you. Girl, you should be all smiles. What's going on?"

Melissa gave her a rueful smile. "I guess I'm getting cold feet."

"Nonsense. You're letting that brain of yours try to figure out everything when you should be following your heart."

Melissa chuckled. "I did that once, and it didn't work out so well."

Sandy shook her head at her and made a clucking noise, "You were a lot younger back then. You're smart and successful now..."

"...and unemployed and homeless for the moment," Melissa added.

Sandy gave her a sour look and then turned and called for reinforcements. "You guys get in here. You're going to have to drag her off to relax."

"What?" Melissa stared, as Jarod and Sam both stepped inside the tent. Her son had a militant look on his little face. Jarod was having a hard time not laughing, as Sam marched right up to her, took the files she was still holding in her hands, and tossed them in the nearest open box.

"Mom we're leaving. Right now. No more dilly-dallying around."

Melissa's smile was barely concealed, as Sam proceeded to treat her the same way she treated him when he was dragging his feet and making their departure for school unnecessarily hard.

"Sam..."

Sam shook his head. "Don't *Sam* me."

Melissa opened her mouth to stop her son from taking his

little game too far and becoming outwardly disrespectful. Before she could say a word, Jarod stepped forward and whispered something in his ear. Sam immediately looked chagrined. He rushed forward and wrapped his arms around her legs.

"Sorry, mom. I didn't mean to be rude. Can we please go now? Jarod promised to get hamburgers and milkshakes to eat on the way there."

"He did?" Melissa asked, hugging Sam close for a moment before releasing him. "That sounds like a good idea since I can't remember eating dinner tonight."

Jarod frowned at her. "You didn't eat? Sam and I dropped off a container of chicken and fries hours ago." He glanced around the tent and then pointed to the white Styrofoam container sitting atop the copier in the corner.

Melissa found it the same time he did and blushed. "I must have set it down and then forgotten about it. I do appreciate the gesture, though."

"I know. You need a break, and we need to hit the road. Sam, grab your mother's bag. I'll make sure she follows." Jarod had already stowed their luggage and the Christmas presents she'd gotten for Sam. She still needed to wrap them, but Jarod had assured her he had plenty of wrapping materials at his place.

"I'll help him put it in the truck," Sandy offered, leaving Melissa and Jarod alone.

Jarod walked over and reached for her hand, searching her eyes as he did so. "Getting cold feet?"

Melissa bit her bottom lip and nodded. "A little."

"Tell me what's bothering you the most," he said, reaching up and tucking a loose strand of hair behind her ear. Her blonde tresses had been left down today. Jarod made a mental note to let her know how much he liked it when she wore her hair this way. This wasn't the moment, but hopefully, in the next few days that would change.

"The unknown?" she murmured after a moment.

Jarod's hand slipped behind her neck as he stepped closer. Melissa's breath paused as her heartbeat accelerated. "The unknown doesn't have to be scary. Let's get one of them out of the way."

He lowered his head and touched his lips to hers. Melissa felt like she'd just grabbed onto a live wire. Tingles rushed through her body and even though the contact only lasted a few seconds, her body felt suddenly alive in a way she'd never before experienced.

Jarod smiled at her. "Wow!"

Melissa couldn't help the small laugh that escaped as she nodded. "You could say that again."

"Wow!" He smiled broadly at her and suddenly the worries that had cast a shadow over the latter part of her day disappeared. She suddenly looked forward to what the week might bring instead of dreading what might go wrong.

"Thank you," she murmured, going up on her tiptoes and placing another brief kiss on his cheek. She dropped back down to her booted feet. "I'm ready to go now. Sandy's probably already trying to keep Sam from coming back in here."

Jarod tucked her hand in his and led her towards the truck. Melissa had decided to leave her vehicle with Sandy. She and Sam would ride up to the mountains in the large tree truck Jarod had driven down. He'd managed to sell all but a handful of trees which had been picked up by a local charity which provided Christmas presents and food to families in need. This year, they would also be getting a live Christmas tree, complete with lights and several boxes of hastily purchased ornaments from a local big-box store.

Melissa hugged Sandy before climbing into the truck. Sam

was already buckled into his car seat which Jarod had installed in the backseat earlier that afternoon. "Ready to go, buddy?"

"Yes!" He pumped a fist into the air.

Melissa chuckled and set about fastening her own seatbelt while Jarod climbed into the driver's seat and did the same. He started up the truck and honked the horn—to Sam's delight—as they pulled out of the parking lot.

"He should calm down after he eats. This is already way past his normal bedtime," Melissa whispered to Jarod, as he navigated the large truck onto Colorado Boulevard.

"I'm not worried. I was thinking we might get on the highway and head toward the foothills. There's not really any place around here where I can pull in and still get out."

"That's probably for the best. The traffic should thin out a bit as well."

"Good." Jarod reached over and turned on the radio. The sound of Christmas carols filled the cab of the truck. He smiled at her and hummed along. When Sam started to sing, albeit a little off-key, Jarod joined along, and Melissa found herself laughing at their antics until her sides hurt.

They reached the outskirts of Denver twenty minutes later. Jarod pulled off the highway and parked the truck next to a fast food restaurant that boasted it stayed open twenty-four hours a day. "So, going through the drive thru is out. How about I go get the food and just bring it back?"

"I could go…," Melissa started to offer, but Jarod stopped her with a shake of his head.

"No need for you to get out in the cold again. I've got this. Sam, buddy…chocolate or strawberry?"

"Chocolate!" Sam replied. "They're the bestest milkshakes

ever."

"Still full of energy," Jarod commented.

"And that's not likely to change if you get him anything other than a small shake," Melissa quietly offered.

"Would you rather he had soda?"

"Uhm...do you want him singing off-key the entire ride?"

"Maybe a small milkshake is the best choice after all," Jarod agreed. "Be right back."

Melissa watched him jog toward the restaurant and then turned back to see Sam watching her with wide, happy eyes.

"Did you have a good day?"

"Yes. Mom?"

"Yes?"

"You like Jarod, right?"

"Jarod's a very nice man...and, yes...I like him."

"Like Sandy likes her husband?"

Melissa hid her surprise and then realized her little boy was growing up and more observant than she'd given him credit for. "Sandy loves her husband."

"So, you love Jarod?" Sam pressed her.

"I...buddy, it's a little too soon to be thinking that way. Love between grownups is...well, it can be complicated."

"Why?"

Yeah, Melissa. Why?

"It...oh, look. Here comes Jarod with our dinner. Try not to spill things all over his truck, okay?"

"I won't."

She reached across the cab and opened Jarod's door, then took the drink carrier from him so he could climb in with the food. She handed Sam his milkshake, pleased that he'd forgotten the line of interrogation he'd been stuck on. At least, for the moment. She was sure he would revisit the topic. Sam was tenacious; he rarely forgot anything.

"I'm going to eat real fast while we're parked here," Jarod told her.

Melissa nodded and then handed Sam a cheeseburger and a small paper packet of fries. She then handed him a napkin and urged him to use it instead of his shirtsleeves, drawing a laugh from Jarod.

She handed Jarod a napkin as well. "Set a good example and don't wipe your fingers on your jeans."

"Yes, ma'am."

She hid the smile that wanted to break free when Jarod dutifully took the napkin and made a big show of wiping his fingers and then his mouth. "That's how it's done, buddy."

Sam duplicated Jarod's actions, wiping his mouth and his fingers and then looking to his mom for a sign of approval. She nodded and then began eating her own food. Jarod finished first and headed the large truck back onto the highway.

"The clerk inside the restaurant said they were getting snow up at the tunnel."

"Is that going to be a problem?" Melissa asked.

"Shouldn't be. The weather report was one of the reasons I wanted to leave tonight. It's supposed to snow from now until tomorrow afternoon."

"When are your parents arriving? Will they be able to fly in?"

"Yeah, they'll get here and instead of me coming back to get them, they're renting an SUV that will fit all of them. It's been a few years, but my dad assures me he remembers how to drive in mountain snow."

"Did you spend a lot of time here when you were a kid?" Melissa asked, remembering that his grandfather had once owned the tree farm where he now lived.

"A bit. My dad spent quite a bit of time here when he was younger. He hasn't been back since the funeral."

"Will coming back here bother him?"

"I don't think so." Jarod glanced in the rearview mirror and then tipped his head for her to look over the seat. Sam had fallen asleep, only half of his cheeseburger being eaten, and most of his fries.

Melissa unbuckled her seatbelt and turned, removing the uneaten food and the milkshake that was mostly empty as well. She readjusted Sam's head and propped it on the sides with the travel pillow she kept with his car seat. She covered him with his favorite blanket and then settled back in her seat.

"He's out."

"Will he sleep again once we get to the farm?"

"He should. I'll have to wake him up to get him inside…"

"…or I can just carry him?"

"Or…we could do that. I stopped being able to carry him very far last summer. He got too heavy and too tall for me to safely manage any steps with him in my arms."

"Well, you won't have to worry about that while I'm around. I'm going to take good care of you and Sam for the next week. Starting right now. There's an extra blanket sitting on the seat next to Sam. Why don't you kick off your boots and try to catch a small

115

nap?" Jarod suggested softly.

"I'm fine," Melissa told him, covering up a yawn with her hands.

"You're exhausted. Humor me and at least get comfortable for the rest of the ride."

"How long will it take us to get to your farm?"

"From here? Another hour and a half, if the weather cooperates. Maybe two hours if they haven't plowed the county road today."

Melissa yawned again. His suggestion of a short nap suddenly sounded like heaven. She reached over the seat for the blanket, toed off her snow boots, and then curled her legs up on the seat, turning slightly toward him in the process.

"Feel better?"

She nodded, forcing her eyes to stay open. "I can talk to you and keep you awake…"

"Or you can give in and close those beautiful eyes," he murmured back, reaching for one of her hands. He rubbed his thumb across the back of her hand, the rhythmic motion lulling her even further into sleep mode. Soon, she couldn't fight to keep her eyes open a moment longer. With a sigh, she relaxed and let her eyes close. The last thing she saw was Jarod smiling tenderly at her. A sight she decided, as she slipped into sleep, she could handle seeing for the rest of her life.

Chapter 14

Two hours later...

Jarod pulled the truck into the large yard and then rubbed his eyes, as he rolled his neck to work the collection of kinks out. The county hadn't plowed the road leading up to his ranch turnoff. It had been snowing steadily all day long. He'd been forced to put the large truck in low gear and move at a snail's pace for the last fifteen grueling miles. His original estimate of an hour and a half had evolved into three hours of tense driving.

He glanced over and smiled at the serene picture Melissa made. She still had the dark bruises beneath her eyes, but her face was relaxed, and a soft smile played around her lips. A glance over the back of the seat showed a still-sleeping Sam. He debated about sitting in the truck a while longer before waking them up, but it was almost two o'clock in the morning and only going to get colder outside.

Turning off the truck, he gently reached out and touched Melissa's shoulder. "Melissa?"

She stirred upon hearing her name and then blinked her eyes several times before awareness filled her eyes. "Hi. I didn't mean to fall asleep..."

"Don't worry about it. We're here. I thought maybe you'd like to go inside and find a bed? It would be a mite more comfortable."

She smiled and then glanced back at her sleeping son. "I need to get Sam inside..."

"I said I would carry him. Let me go unlock the door and turn the porch light on. You can go on inside. I'll bring Sam and then come back for your bags."

117

"Are you sure? I can't help..."

"Melissa," Jarod reached out and brushed a strand of hair off her cheek. "Go inside."

She nodded and then opened the door, letting a blast of cold air into the truck's cab. "Brrrr. It's much colder here than in Denver."

"We're approximately four thousand feet higher, and it's been snowing all day." Jarod quickly exited the truck and hurried up the porch steps. He opened the front door, switched on the porch light, and then stamped his feet a time or two before striding directly to the fireplace that sat center stage in the large room. Minutes later, a fire blazed in the hearth.

Jarod hated coming home to a cold cabin. He'd made sure the hearth contained logs and an adequate amount of fire-starter materials before he ever left for any length of time. When he heard the sound of footsteps behind him, he turned to see Melissa standing in the doorway. Her eyes were filled with wide-eyed wonder.

He glanced around at the various animal heads displayed on the walls, the large stone column of the fireplace that rose to the ceiling, and the natural logs that comprised the walls of the cabin. A second glance at Melissa told him his home was not what she'd been expecting.

Deciding to leave that conversation for a later time, he walked toward her. "Have a seat by the fireplace. I'll go get Sam and your bags."

"Oh." Melissa shook her head, as if to pull herself from a momentary trance, and started to turn after him. Jarod intercepted her with a shake of his head.

"Get warm. I'll be right back."

He jogged down the steps, thankful that they faced sunward in the afternoons and the recent snows had mostly melted. The back steps were a different story. He kept a large tub of a snow-melt product right inside the doorway to prevent them from icing over. He opened the rear passenger door and quickly unhooked the straps that had kept Sam upright for the last part of their journey.

Sam started to stir, but Jarod shushed him as he slid him from the car seat and into his arms. He grabbed his coat to drape across Sam's back and then carried him inside. Melissa was standing in front of the fire, her hands extended as her eyes roamed around his living space. He headed for the hallway to his right and stopped at the first bedroom.

He didn't bother to turn the light on, the large skylight in the ceiling provided enough moonlight for his task. He laid Sam down but, before he could slip the child's boots off, Melissa was there to get her son ready for a restful night's sleep.

Jarod watched her for a minute and then backed out of the bedroom, murmuring, "I'll go get our bags."

He took a few minutes to gather up their belongings from the truck and then locked it up for the night. He set everything down next to the door and then stirred the fire and added another log for good measure. The sound of footsteps in the hallway had him turning and watching as Melissa came toward him. She had a soft smile on her face. Jarod was sure he'd never seen anything as beautiful.

She looked happier than he'd ever seen her, and Jarod knew in that moment that bringing her here was the right thing to do. He held out a hand to her, pleased when she placed her own in it. "Tired?"

"Very," Melissa told him with a soft laugh.

"Hungry?" he then asked, smoothing the back of her knuckles with his thumb.

"Not really." She paused and then asked, "Are you? I could make..."

Jarod pulled her hand and then shook his head. "I'm fine."

He pulled her close and hugged her for a moment, not releasing her until he felt her body relax and her breathing evened out. He pushed her a few inches away and asked, "How about I get your bags to your room?"

Melissa nodded and then covered her face with her hands as she tried to hide a yawn. "Sorry."

"Don't be," he assured her. "Let's get you settled for the night." He picked up her bags and then directed her down the hallway to the bedroom just beyond the one where Sam slept. This bedroom had a private bath attached to it. He set her bags down at the foot of the bed.

He turned and saw her standing just inside the doorway, taking in the handmade quilt, the pine furniture, and the wooden rocking chair in the corner. "There are towels in the bathroom closet. If you get cold, you can adjust the heat by either turning on the heater, or I can light the fireplace."

One of the best features of this cabin was the real fireplace contained in each of the rooms. Jarod didn't normally use this room and therefore, he didn't have anything in this room with which to start a fire. For Melissa, he would gladly correct that omission.

She came further into the room and then smiled at him, "I don't need a fire in here. I'm not used to having a live fireplace. I would be afraid of catching the place on fire."

Jarod smiled and shook his head, "I'm sure you'd be fine. I'll teach you how to make a proper fire tomorrow, if you like."

"I would like that." She yawned and swayed on her feet. Jarod turned and headed for the bedroom door, stopping for a moment when she was right in front of him.

"Get some sleep. Don't worry about waking up at a certain

time."

"You obviously haven't spent much time with a little boy. There is no such thing as sleeping in with Sam around. He'll be wide awake first thing tomorrow."

"Then he and I will amuse ourselves. I want you to get some rest. We both know you need it." He searched her tired eyes for a moment and then moved toward her, crowding her when she didn't back up. "I need to check something out."

She met his gaze and whispered, "What is that?"

"This," he murmured just before he settled his lips over her own. He used one hand to cup the back of her neck, as he angled her head for a deeper taste than earlier that same evening. This kiss was just as surprising, sending a warm feeling coursing through his body and his heart racing.

Melissa's arms came up and wrapped around his neck, going up on her tiptoes and leaning against him.

After several long moments, Jarod broke their kiss, putting little butterfly kisses on her cheeks and her nose before leaning back, so that he could look in to her eyes. "That was pretty wonderful."

Melissa gave him a soft smile and nodded. "What was the word you used earlier? Wow?"

Jarod brushed his thumb over her bottom lip and nodded, "Wow! I just needed to make sure I wasn't imaging the extent of Wow from earlier." He kissed her once more and then released her and, with a whistle, headed for the bedroom door.

"Jarod?" she called after him, turning and staring at him with wide eyes.

"Yes?"

"Did you? Imagine it?" she asked softly.

Jarod let a broad smile fill his face, and he shook his head.

"Not even a bit."

She blushed and then smiled back at him. "Me neither."

"Goodnight, beautiful. I'll see you in, well…since it's already morning, I'll see you around noon." He pulled the door shut and then went through the cabin, checking doors and windows and banking the fire in the front room. His own bedroom was on the other side of the kitchen. He quickly went through the motions of getting ready to sleep, setting his alarm for six o'clock so that he wouldn't risk having Sam wake up and go searching for his mother.

Melissa was going to rest and relax while she was here with him. A small foretaste of what her life could be like if she consented to moving here and making a life with him. He intended to pamper her and help make her decision an easy one when the time came. But first, he needed to get some much-needed sleep. Keeping up with Sam was going to be a whole new dimension to his normally quiet and sane life. One he was actually looking forward to.

***

Joy hovered in the large room of Jarod's cabin, enjoying the way the shadows played on the walls as the fire in the hearth slowly died to a small glow of embers. Angels didn't feel cold, but there was something comforting about a fire.

She looked around Jarod's home, wondering how her young charge would react when he woke up in the morning. She moved down the hallway and checked on Sam, pleased to see that he was sleeping soundly. He and his mother both needed rest. Joy was pleased to know that Jarod had made that his goal for the next few days.

Melissa hadn't really been able to fully relax since before she'd given birth to Sam. Joy hadn't really broken the angel code, but she had done a little bit of research on Melissa's past. It saddened her to think about how alone the young woman had become. The demands of providing for herself and her child had consumed her at times. Even more recently, when she'd thought she had a secure position in the city government, she hadn't allowed herself to relax. It was time she discovered the joy of taking a walk in the woods, watching a sunset, or sleeping in on a Saturday morning.

Joy left Sam's room to return to the front room, frowning when she realized there wasn't anything that made the cabin feel or look like Christmas was only a few days away. Four days to be exact. There was no time to waste if Sam was going to have the best Christmas ever.

Joy looked around, wondering how she could help Jarod remember what was missing. She found a photo album sitting on the shelf. She carefully looked through the pages, finally finding exactly what she needed. A picture of Jarod with his parents and his two sisters, gathered around a lovely Christmas tree.

She carefully removed the picture from the album and then surveyed the room, wondering where she could leave the picture that Jarod would find it. She finally decided to leave it lying on the floor, right in the middle of the walkway where it would clearly be seen. She hadn't exactly broken any rules, she hadn't planted any thoughts or whispered any suggestions to Jarod. She hadn't manipulated anyone's emotions. She'd just left a little clue to do that for her. Real memories carried powerful emotions and, since everyone in the picture was smiling, she hoped the memory would be pleasant and one he wanted to recreate with Melissa and Sam.

Satisfied that things were still headed in the right direction, she ascended back up to heaven just in time for choir practice. She smiled at Hope and Faith as she took her place, wondering how things were going for them. Since they were at practice and not still down on earth helping their charges, things must be going well. That made her smile.

"Alright, angels. There's only a few more days to practice. I know we've done this before…"

"Some of us have sung these songs for thousands of years,"

one of the elder angels called out, drawing chuckles and nods of agreement from most of the choir.

"That may be. However, we are heralding the Christmas Season. For humans, this is a yearly reminder of the love our Father has for them. After all, we are celebrating the birth of His Son." The choir master turned and addressed the orchestra for a moment. After getting affirmative nods from all of the instrumentalists, he turned back to the angel choir.

"Now, can we begin at the chorus? We'll be doing all seven verses, but the chorus is so full of joy; I'd like to begin there."

The choir master raised his hands, and with a count of four, he lowered them, and the heavens were filled with the sound of angelic singing, five-part harmonies, and celebration. Approximately two thousand years had passed since Jesus had arrived on the earth as a human infant. It was the single most important event in the history of the world, because it was the beginning of the redemption plan designed to provide a way for humankind to once again have communion with their Creator.

"Alleluia! Alleluia! Alleu! Alleu! Alleu! Alleluia!"

The choir master lowered his hands as the majestic sound faded away, smiling serenely when a bright light arose from the palace on the hillside, situated right in the middle of Heaven. It seems their efforts had drawn the attention of the throne room.

"Wonderful! That is all for now. I will see you all back here tomorrow, if your duties allow for that. Have a blessed day."

Joy took her time leaving the choir hall, looking around for her friends, but it seemed they had already gone their separate ways. With nothing to do and no place to be for several hours, she headed off to the recreation center. While her human charge was sleeping, she was going to partake in an angel game or two to pass the time.

Chapter 15

"Listen," Jarod told Sam, cocking his head to the right as he searched for the noise once more. Smiling, he nodded and told his young companion, "Your mother is finally awake." A glance at the clock on the mantle showed it was nearly two o'clock in the afternoon. Jarod had set a time of three o'clock for her to wake up, or he was going to have to intervene and start the process.

"Yay! Can we make her pancakes now?" Sam asked, jumping off the couch and heading for the kitchen. True to Melissa's prediction, Sam had been wide awake by seven o'clock and ready for breakfast. Jarod had already showered and dressed by the time a sleepy-eyed Sam had wandered from his assigned bedroom, in search of a bathroom.

Jarod had shown him the small three quarter bath directly across the hall and then set about getting pancake batter started. Sam had been a great helper, even managing to flip the smaller pancakes all by himself. It was obvious he'd helped his mother in the kitchen numerous times, and it was something he enjoyed.

"Let's go and see if we can catch her while she's still in bed," Jarod suggested.

He retrieved the batter from the fridge and a few minutes later, he was scooping three perfectly rounded pancakes onto a plate. Sam had retrieved the glass of orange juice he'd poured earlier and had then added butter and syrup to the tray that had been left sitting on the counter for just this purpose.

Sam looked at the tray and then clapped his hands. "It's ready."

"How about I carry it, and you open the doors for me? Be sure to knock before you just open the door and barge in. We don't want to embarrass your mother," Jarod cautioned him.

Sam nodded and then headed down the hallway, stopping at the closed door and rapping his knuckles on the door three times in rapid succession. He counted to three and then rapped two more times.

"That's our secret code," he told Jarod proudly.

"Good to know," Jarod commented, holding the tray steady.

"Come in," Melissa's soft voice called out.

Sam opened the door and then rushed to the side of the bed. His mother had obviously crawled back beneath the covers, whether right after taking care of nature's call, or in response to the knock on the door. She was sitting up against the headboard, the quilt spread across her lap, a serene smile on her face

Sam climbed up on the bed and hugged her tightly before bouncing and telling her in an outside voice, "We made you breakfast."

Melissa winced and covered her ears, reminding her son, "Inside voice, please."

"Does your head hurt?" Jarod asked softly, coming forward and setting the tray down on the side table. "I can get you some aspirin, or I have Excedrin if you need it?"

"I think I'm just a little dehydrated. Maybe some water?" she murmured to him, looking at the tray and then her son. "Did you help Jarod make me breakfast?"

"Uh-huh. I flipped some of the pancakes all by myself, but Jarod did those. I ate the ones I made."

Melissa hid a smile and then commented, "Well, a good chef always tastes his work. Maybe you can make my pancakes next time."

"They were really yummy. Eat mom, and then Jarod said we could take a drive around the trees."

"That sounds fun. Can I have a shower first?"

"You can take as much time as you need," Jarod informed her, handing her a tall glass of water and then setting the tray on her lap. "Anything else I can get you?"

Melissa shook her head and then listened as Sam began to talk about all of the things he and Jarod had done while she was sleeping. She made the appropriate responses, and giving Jarod sideways looks as if to ask if he was sorry he'd brought them up here yet.

"He's a very active little boy, but I already knew that."

Once Melissa was finished eating, Jarod removed the tray and then suggested to Sam, "Let's go find your snow gear while your mom gets showered and dressed. There's only a few hours of daylight left, and I realized this morning we are missing something really big."

"We are?" Sam asked, a frown marring his brow. "What are we missing?"

Jarod made a face and then lowered his voice, "Promise not to tell anyone?"

Sam's eyes lit up at the thought of being told a secret and he nodded and crossed his heart with his fingers. "I promise."

Jarod leaned closer and whispered, "I own a Christmas tree farm, but I don't even have a Christmas tree in my house yet."

He honestly hadn't given a thought to getting a tree for his own space. Prior to taking his trees to Denver, he'd been planning to catch a flight to visit his parents for a few days. That had all changed after meeting Melissa and Sam, but he'd been in Denver when his plans changed, so he hadn't given any thought to how his home

127

looked. Completely undecorated.

That had all changed when he'd woken up and headed to light a fire in the main room. He'd found a picture lying on the floor, just below the photo album where it should have been safely stored.

The picture was one from his childhood. A family photo taken on a Christmas morning when he was eight or nine years old. Almost the same age as Sam was this year. Everyone had been in their pajamas, telling Jarod that the picture had been taken shortly after the gifts had been opened that morning. It had brought back such happy memories, but then he'd looked around the front room and realized there would be no similar memories happening this year unless he got his act together.

He had houseguests, and his family was enroute. Christmas was just a few days away and that meant he was going to need Sam and Melissa's help to get his house ready. There were decorations to be put up, lights to be strung on the front porch, wreaths to make, a tree to find and decorate, and he hadn't even given a thought to Christmas dinner yet.

The first thing on the agenda was getting a tree and then decorating it this evening with some help from two people who were quickly becoming very important to him. He felt blessed to have this time with them, and he intended to make it a Christmas they all remembered.

Sam looked concerned and then raced from the bedroom to check for himself. He came back a moment later with a grave look on his face, "Santa's not going to be very happy with you."

"I know. I was wondering if maybe you and your mom could help me pick out the best Christmas tree on the lot and help me decorate it tonight?" He turned to Melissa and told her, "I put a pot of chili on the stove for supper."

Melissa smiled at him. "That sounds really nice. With

everything going on, I didn't even think about our Christmas tree this year. Thank you."

"No problem. Sam, let's go get you suited up. Finding the perfect Christmas tree is hard work."

"I'm good at finding the right tree. Aren't I, mom?"

"The best. I'll get ready fast."

"No hurry. We'll be out front when you're ready." Jarod gave her a wink, wishing Sam wasn't around, so he could indulge his desire to give her a good morning kiss. They hadn't talked about open displays of affection when Sam was around, and Jarod refused to do anything that might cross a line he didn't know about. He'd never dated a woman with a child, but he'd read plenty of articles and seen enough social media posts to know that it had its own set of rules that single women didn't have to think about.

Jarod respected Melissa and had quickly fallen in love with her son. He wouldn't willingly do anything that might upset that or damage his chances of a future with them by his side. Jarod already suspected that Melissa and Sam were the missing pieces to his family puzzle. He just needed to move slowly and not push too fast. Melissa was already nervous about where they were headed. His sole job was to put her at ease and make sure this was the best Christmas she and her son had ever had.

***

Joy somersaulted over the snow-covered trees, celebrating the fact that her little clue had done its job. Jarod had not only remembered he needed a Christmas tree; he'd remembered all of the other accoutrements that the holiday needed. Her little plan had worked better than she could have even imagined.

She was so happy! She heard the sound of a bird and looked up to see an eagle soaring overhead. She flew up and joined him, following his every turn and dip. He approached the mountains and soon a rock ledge that bore a large nest.

Joy held back as she watched two little eaglets answer his call, welcoming him back to the nest with exuberance. Their mother had been keeping watch from a ledge above the nest, and with a call to her mate, she soared off in search of more food for herself and her babies.

Joy let out a happy sigh and then floated back down to observe Sam and the hunt for the perfect Christmas tree. She loved this time of the year and seeing the bright smile on Sam's face this morning made her feel even more confident that his wishes were going to come true. Jarod and Melissa were making her job so easy. She looked forward to sitting back and watching the romance between them unfold.

Chapter 16

Melissa was in love with the place Jarod called home! Everywhere she looked there were piles of snow, pine trees with boughs bearing the remains of yesterday's storm, and a crisp blue sky above. Small animal tracks could be seen moving through the rows of trees. Off in the distance, she could hear the call of birds who had remained in the area through the winter.

"You keeping up?" Jarod asked, slowing his pace while Sam raced ahead.

"I am. Jarod, your home is amazing! I've been to the mountains before, but this place…it's almost like a fairytale."

"Wait until you see the town and the area where they want to set up the tourist center. It's like something out of a Hollywood movie set."

"I can't wait to see it. Thank you for bringing us here and sharing your holiday with us. Sam is having a great time."

"He's a great kid. How about his mom? Is she having a great time?"

"Well, let's see. She got to sleep until two o'clock in the afternoon. Was served breakfast in bed that consisted of the perfect food—pancakes. She's now walking outside in one of the most beautiful places she could imagine with her son and a handsome man... I think things are off to a great start."

Jarod smiled and then leaned down to whisper next to her ear. "I think you forgot something."

"Really?" she arched a brow at him.

He nodded and then pulled her to a stop, moved in front of her and placed a quick kiss on her lips. He then settled back by her

131

side, pretending as if nothing had happened. "Good morning."

"Good afternoon. What was that?" she asked, touching her lips.

"Well, I wanted to kiss you earlier, when we brought you breakfast, but we haven't discussed Sam, and I didn't want to do anything that might make things uncomfortable for you."

"Oh! Thank you," she murmured, looking chagrined. "To be honest, I've not dated, so I haven't even considered Sam and how this might affect him."

"I just wasn't sure if you were okay with PDA's around him or not," Jarod murmured.

"PDA's? Sounds like we're back in junior high school. Sam is very affectionate. Honestly, I don't know how he'll react. I guess I don't really know how to answer that question right now."

Jarod nodded and then asked, "Would you be okay with me holding your hand where he could see?"

Melissa shrugged and then nodded, "I think so."

"Good." Jarod removed his glove and then reached for her hand, removing her own and tucking it into his own pocket. "Let me know if your hand gets cold."

Melissa chuckled, but the tingles from where their palms touched felt so good, she couldn't fault his actions. Holding his gloved hand wouldn't have been nearly as fun.

"Mom! Jarod! I found it!" Sam called from up ahead.

Jarod grinned and then pulled her with him as he increased his pace. They found Sam standing in front of a tall tree, possibly twenty feet tall, with a base of boughs that were at least eight feet in diameter.

"Wow! Sam, that's some tree," Melissa told him. "Don't you

think it's a bit big for Jarod's house?"

Sam put his hands on his hips and tipped his head back, straining to see the top of the tree. "Well…maybe just a bit."

"More than a bit, Sam," Jarod added. "This tree is many feet too tall for my front room, and it's also one of the few trees that were here when I took over the tree farm and not one I ever plan to cut down. My grandfather planted this tree when he bought this land. Every time I look at it, I'm reminded of him. Let's keep looking."

Sam nodded and off he went, calling out to them time and again, but each time there was something about the tree that made it unsuitable for Jarod's home. Finally, after twenty minutes of walking amongst the rows of trees, they found Sam just standing and staring at the perfect seven-foot tall tree. It was perfectly shaped on all sides, had thick needles with plenty of branches, and the perfect spire at the top for setting a star or angel upon.

"It's perfect," Melissa told him, placing her hands upon Sam's shoulders.

"Jarod, is this the tree?" Sam asked, looking up with hope in his eyes.

"Buddy, this is the perfect tree. Great job. Wanna help me cut it down?"

"Sure!"

Melissa stood back and watched as Jarod and Sam worked together to cut the tree down. Sam had missed having a male role model in his life, and she'd often felt bad about that. Watching Jarod with her son now, she realized she couldn't have dreamed up a better role model or a more kind and compassionate man to show her son what he'd been missing. Jarod was patient and, even though Sam talked non-stop, Jarod never seemed to grow tired of having the little boy around. Sam's biological father had grown tired of him months before he'd even been born.

Why couldn't Sam have had a father like Jarod? Why couldn't I have married a man like Jarod the first time?

It was in that moment that Melissa was honest with herself, acknowledging that she'd been holding back for fear that she might fall in love with someone Sam disliked. Rather, it seemed that Sam and she had similar tastes. If her son didn't already love Jarod, he was definitely close. As for herself, she was ready to see exactly where a future with Jarod would lead. Hopefully to the fulfillment of all of her dreams and his. She just needed to conquer her fear of the unknown and take that final leap of faith.

"Mom, did you see? I worked the saw and everything." Sam rushed up to her.

"I did see that." She looked over at Jarod and mouthed her thanks. She'd been able to give Jarod of lot of experiences but cutting down a Christmas tree wasn't one of them. In fact, Melissa didn't even own a saw, let alone know where one would go in Denver to perform such a feat.

Jarod merely tipped his chin at her and then picked up the trunk of the tree and started dragging it back to the small ATV they'd used to drive out to the rows of trees. He put it on top of the vehicle and then secured it with a long piece of rope before announcing they needed to head back before the sun went down behind the mountains.

Melissa glanced up and guessed they probably only had half-an-hour, at the most, although a full moon had already risen in the sky. A part of her wondered how the trees would look bathed in moonlight.

"Penny for your thoughts," Jarod murmured, as he helped Sam fastened his seatbelt.

"I was just looking at the moon and wondering what it must look like out here at night."

"Amazing," Jarod told her. "Maybe we can come out here

tomorrow night…"

Melissa shook her head, as she explained, "I wouldn't feel right leaving Sam alone in your cabin."

"My parents and siblings will be here tomorrow. I'm sure they wouldn't mind keeping an eye on him for a little while. It's supposed to be a clear sky tomorrow, and I can guarantee you've never seen stars like you can see them out here."

Melissa bit her bottom lip and then nodded. "If you're sure they wouldn't mind, that sounds like fun."

"I'll arrange it then. Let's get back. Sam can help me put the stand on the tree if you can handle the cornbread. It's nothing too hard, just a mix you add water to."

"That's the only kind of cornbread I ever make. It tastes just as good as the other stuff and doesn't require emptying out the pantry to make."

"A woman who thinks like I do. Whatever shall I do?" he asked, winking at her as he walked around to get in on the driver's side. She got into her seat and then smiled at Sam. "Having fun?"

"Yes." He couldn't have given her a brighter grin. On their way back to the cabin, Jarod pointed out various things, including some deer that were taking advantage of the feed that had been placed atop the snow.

"You feed the deer?" she asked.

"On years when we have lots of snow, I work with the Division of Wildlife to provide food for the herds that winter here. They've been assisting in feeding the wildlife for decades. It was one of the first things I did when I moved here. I like being able to give back a little."

"What about hunters?"

"It's way past the last hunting season for this area. My lands bump against the wilderness preserve, and there is never any hunting inside of that area."

"Sounds like you have the perfect piece of land," she told him. Everything she'd seen and heard about Jarod's property had only served to confirm what her eyes told her; Jarod's Christmas tree farm was unlike anything else she'd ever seen. If Christmas Valley was even half as put together and special, the community definitely had the means to put on an unforgettable tourist attraction.

Chapter 17

"Do you need any help in the kitchen?" Jarod asked.

"I don't think so." They had reached the cabin, so Melissa headed inside to start the cornbread. Working in Jarod's kitchen was like a dream. He had all of the latest appliances and, for a bachelor, his cupboards were very organized. He'd even labeled some of the shelves.

Melissa placed the pan of cornbread in the oven and then she scrambled for her phone as it rang. She answered it on the third ring, smiling when she saw the caller I.D. was her friend.

"Sandy!"

"Melissa, I hope I'm not interrupting anything, but I wanted to make sure you got there okay and that things were going well."

"Things are going more than well. Jarod's place is fabulous. Sam is having so much fun, and Jarod has been the perfect host."

"Sounds like Sam's not the only one having a good time. You and Jarod must be getting along."

"We are. Sandy, I know it's early yet, but everything about this place—Jarod, the way he is with Sam and me—I could see myself getting used to this. Am I crazy for thinking this way so soon?"

"Hon, when you meet that special person, you just know it. I've known you and Jarod were right for one another since the first time you two met. He's the real deal, Melissa. Don't be afraid of putting your heart out there. Something tells me the last thing that man would ever do is drop it."

Melissa thought about the way she felt when Jarod kissed her, and her heartbeat sped up and excitement surged through her veins.

He was everything she'd ever wanted in a man and, so far, she'd not been able to come up with one thing she didn't like about him. Not one.

"Mom, we're ready to decorate the tree," Sam hollered out, as held the front door so that Jarod could bring the tree in.

"Is that Sam in the background?" Sandy asked.

"Yes. We cut down a Christmas tree a little while ago and they just finished putting the stand on it. Can you believe with everything going on, I didn't even think about a tree?"

Sandy's chuckle came through the phone. "With everything that's been on your plate, I'm surprised you haven't forgotten more things. Have you thought that not having the festival to drive you crazy next December might allow you to actually enjoy Christmas again?"

"I enjoy Christmas." Melissa frowned.

"No, you stress to make Christmas special for Sam the few days you have before Christmas because the festival sucks up all of your time and energy."

Melissa didn't even try to reply. Sandy was correct. No matter how many times she told herself she was going to prepare for Christmas ahead of time, the festival took priority. She was always racing against the calendar to make Christmas special once the festival ended. At least this year she'd done her shopping early. Last year she'd been fighting the crowds at the local mall on December twenty-third. She'd promised herself that was never going to happen again.

She watched Jarod and Sam carrying boxes of decorations from a hall closet and smiled. "I should probably go," she told Sandy. "Is everything…"

"Don't even go there," Sandy warned her. "I'm personally not setting foot back in the office until the twenty-eighth. If there is a problem, they can call Mayor Brown with it."

Melissa laughed, trying to imagine the mayor actually receiving such a call and being expected to actually deal with it. "I think that would be an exercise in futility. I don't think the man actually knows how to do anything. He just likes to throw his weight around. He'd tell maintenance to handle it."

"Well, neither one of us are going to worry about what's happening. Go enjoy decorating the tree with your son and that handsome man who couldn't keep his eyes off of you yesterday. If I don't talk to you again, Merry Christmas."

"Merry Christmas to you as well. See you after the New Year." Melissa quickly added, "And thanks for calling."

"You bet you will. That's what friends do. Bye."

"Bye." Melissa disconnected the call and then slipped her phone back onto the counter. Talking with Sandy was always good for her mental state. She'd learned over the last few years that Sandy had a knack for seeing how things really were before most people did. Sandy had seen something of value in Jarod from his arrival in Denver. Melissa was now seeing that same thing, and she realized she was quickly falling for the man. If she wasn't careful, she might even be tempted to use the "L" word where he was concerned.

Chapter 18

Jarod watched Melissa and Sam, as they helped put his ornaments on the tree. Sam had been very eager to help with the stand. It had become very apparent that the young boy was missing interaction with an adult male. Jarod wanted to be that role model. The feeling had been building for the last several days, but now that Sam was here in his home, he had so many things he wanted to show and teach him.

And there was his mother. Melissa looked happier right now than he'd ever seen her. She was smiling, laughing and teasing both of them. For the first time since they'd met, the bruising beneath her eyes was almost gone. Being here in Christmas Valley was good for her. And for him.

Jarod loved living here but, since he'd arrived, he'd always felt as if something was missing. Today, that feeling had been nonexistent. Could it be that he'd been missing Melissa and Sam? His cabin finally felt like a real home.

"Jarod, what do you normally put on the top of the tree?" Melissa asked him. She was sitting on the floor in front of the fire, a box of ornaments open in front of her. She was placing the hooks on the ornaments and then Sam was carefully and thoughtfully placing them on the branches.

"There should be a star in one of these boxes," he stated, examining the plastic boxes from the closet for a moment and then selecting one and removing the lid. He smiled as he silently congratulated himself for having selected the correct box the first time around. "Here it is."

"Oh! That's really pretty," Melissa told him. "Where did you find something so unique?"

Jarod looked at the stained glass star and grinned, "They make them right here in Christmas Valley. I'll introduce you to the artisan if you like."

"I would most definitely like." She took the star when he offered it, turning it around several times and watching the firelight play off the various swirls of color that were cast around the room. "This is truly a work of art."

"I thought so," he agreed. He took the star back and then addressed Sam, "Want to help me put it on the tree?"

Sam eagerly nodded, so Jarod walked over to the three-step ladder and climbed up to the top. The star was heavier than most tree toppers, but it had been designed so that it was supported by several branches instead of one.

"Can you hold this for me?" Jarod asked Sam, handing him the star and watching as the little boy held it so carefully. Jarod arranged the branches at the very top of the tree, and then he reached down for the star. "Okay, here goes."

Jarod situated the star over the branches and then carefully threaded the cord down the back of the tree until he reached the extension cord which he'd placed there earlier, just for this purpose. Once the star was stable, he climbed down the small ladder and then reached around the back of the tree for the power strip.

"Sam, would you like to do the honors?"

"Wait!"

Jarod frowned, "Did I forget something?"

Melissa shook her head. "No, I just always turn the lights down so that we can truly appreciate the tree."

Jarod smiled. "My mother always did the same." He reached for the light switch, flipping it down and bathing the room in the soft glow from the fire. "Okay, Sam. Now we're ready."

Sam nodded and then asked, "Mom, can you count for me."

"Sure," Melissa agreed. "One. Two. Three."

Sam flipped the switch, and Jarod was unable to take his eyes off of Melissa as she stared in delight at the decorated tree.

"It's gorgeous," she murmured.

"Yes, gorgeous," Jarod returned, talking about her and not the tree.

Melissa turned her head and then quirked a brow at him. "Were you looking at the tree?"

Jarod shook his head and then murmured for her ears alone, "I couldn't take my eyes off of you."

"I'm not nearly as fun to look at as this Christmas tree."

"You let me be the judge of that," Jarod told her.

"If you like," she murmured, and Jarod was sure he saw a blush on her cheeks.

He leaned toward her and whispered for her ears alone, "I like." He then turned to see what Sam was doing, only to find the little boy curled up in the oversized chair, his eyes slowly closing with each passing moment. Jarod tipped his head for Melissa and watched as her expression went soft and tender.

"He's tired. He had a big day."

"Want me to carry him to bed?" Jarod offered.

"No. He needs to brush his teeth and wash up a bit." She walked over and squatted down in front of the chair. "Sam? Hey, buddy. It's time for bed."

"Uh huh," Sam murmured with a nod.

"Let's go get ready and find your pajamas," she told him. Jarod watched as she lovingly escorted him down the hallway, talking softly to him all the while. Jarod began packing up the ornament boxes, stowed them back in the closet, and then he headed down the hallway to find out how things were progressing.

Melissa was sitting on the side of the bed, rubbing her hand in circles on Sam's back as she finished telling him a story about reindeer and snowmen. "Sleep tight," she whispered in his ear as his eyes closed, and she retreated from the bed.

Jarod backed up and waited as she slid the bedroom door closed. He reached for her hand and led her toward the back porch doors. He handed her a sheepskin coat to put on, neither of them saying anything to disturb the mood.

He led her to the porch railing and just waited for her to respond. She looked up at the sky, the Milky Way was visible in all of its splendor. "Amazing, isn't it?" he whispered.

"I've never seen so many stars," she commented, gazing up at the sky.

"It's even more beautiful out amongst the trees."

She glanced at him and then nodded. "I can't wait to see them tomorrow." She covered up a yawn with a hand and then chuckled softly. "Guess it's bedtime for me, as well."

"Want to help me finish decorating in the morning?"

"I'd love to. Mind if I use your kitchen to bake cookies?"

"Not at all. I should have everything you need and, if not, we can run into town and grab it from the store. It's only a fifteen minute drive in if we cut around the backside of Lake Dillon."

"It seems impossible that civilization is so close. Yet, it feels like we're in the middle of nowhere."

"I told you Christmas Valley was special. I can't wait to show it to you. "

"It most certainly is unique. I can't wait to see everything. Goodnight."

She turned to go back inside the house, but Jarod stopped her for a moment. He gently tipped her chin up and placed a tender kiss there. "Until tomorrow."

She touched her lips and then nodded once before slipping indoors.

Jarod remained where he was, silently offering up a request to the heaven.

She's here, God. Thank you for keeping us safe on the drive up and for bringing Melissa and Sam into my life. Help her continue to see how perfect this setting is for herself and her child.

Give me wisdom and Help me be preferred when she thinks about the future.

I love you, Father God. I trust you to help direct my paths and to lead me in the direction You would have me to go. Amen.

His prayer finished, Jarod took one last look at the stars and then headed inside He banked the various fires and then headed for his bedroom. After a quick shower, he immediately fell into a restful sleep.

Chapter 19

The next day was filled with activity. Upon waking, Melissa found Sam and Jarod already scrambling eggs and cooking bacon. Once again, she'd slept way past her normal time. She felt badly about Jarod having to watch over Sam.

"I'll start setting my alarm, so that I'm awake before him," she offered.

Jarod gave her a puzzled look, as he asked, "Why would you do that? You're supposed to be relaxing."

"But Sam is my responsibility, and I feel like I should be up…"

"Hush," Jarod told her with a smile and a shake of his head. "I'm not complaining. Frankly, I kind of like having that time with him. He's so calm. This morning, he crawled up to sit next to me on the couch, and we just talked."

"He did? What did you talk about?" Melissa tried not to sound concerned, but Sam was an open book and didn't seem to have any filter over his thoughts or his words at this age. There was no telling what he'd choose to tell someone like Jarod.

Jarod picked up on her concern and chuckled. "Nothing too bad, I promise. Sam likes to talk, and I discovered this morning that his words don't always match what he's thinking about."

Melissa nodded and chuckled herself. "He changes topics like the wind and even I have trouble keeping up with him at times."

"Mom!"

Melissa turned her head to see Sam standing a short distance away, dressed and carrying his snow gear. "What's up, Sam? You look like you're ready to go outside."

145

"We're going into town. Come on, you have to get dressed."

"We're going into town?" she asked Jarod.

"I thought we could get some more groceries. You can check out the pantry before we leave and tell me what else we need for the baking you talked about doing, and I wanted to show you the shops in town."

"The same shops that want to band together for the tourists?" she asked.

"The same ones."

"Jarod, do these shopkeepers know they would have to change things up to meet the expectations of tourists who would be willing to drive up here?"

Jarod smirked and then stood up, pulling her up beside him. "Why don't you wait to make those assumptions until we return from town? I think you're going to be pleasantly surprised."

Melissa arched a brow and then shrugged. "Okay. Let me go get dressed, and we can leave in say, thirty minutes?"

"That's too long," Sam whined at her, only to have Jarod clear his throat and shake his head in reprimand. Sam's shoulders sagged and then he brightened, "Thirty minutes. But hurry, please?"

"I'll do my very best to be ready in twenty-nine minutes. Will that do?"

Sam grinned, "Make it twenty-eight, and I'll be a happy camper all day long."

Melissa tousled his hair. "Done."

She quickly dressed for walking around the shops in jeans, a turtleneck, topped by a heavy button-up shirt, and then pulled her hair up and tucked it beneath a knit snowcap. She grabbed her gloves, scarf, and winter jacket, and then went to find the boys.

They were peering into the pantry with puzzled looks upon their faces. "Problems?"

Jarod looked relieved to see her and quietly offered, "Sam says you always make gingerbread and was concerned that we wouldn't have the right ingredients. He seemed to think that everyone knew what those were. I must confess, I enjoy eating it but have no clue as to what goes into it."

Melissa giggled. "Lucky for both of you, I do. My secret...a pre-made cookie pouch."

"They make those?" Jarod inquired.

Melissa stepped back and nodded. "There are all sorts of short cuts available now. Is this a big grocery store or just a little necessity one?"

"I thought we would drive into Silverthorne and visit the big grocery store on our way home. Sam and I decided that my freezer is sadly lacking ice cream and that must be rectified."

"Unfortunately, ice cream is one of his favorite foods."

"Mine too," Jarod agreed. "Sam, go get your boots, and we'll get out of here." They headed for the rack by the front door where their winter gear was stowed and he offered, "My parents called a while ago. They plan to be here around two o'clock this afternoon. Two of my sisters will be coming in later as their flight was delayed. They were planning to rent their own vehicle anyway, so they will be here sometime this evening around nine."

Melissa's mind went into planning mode. "Do we need to make up beds for them? What about dinner? We should probably pick up something while we're at the store. I can get it going when we get back..."

Jarod placed a hand over her mouth and shook his head. "Slow down. You're here to relax. Dinner is already taken care of. I set steaks out this morning to thaw. I have plenty of potatoes we can pop into the oven to bake, and canned vegetables we can reheat when the time comes. The only thing we might pick up are some dinner rolls."

"Or we can pick up the frozen dough and bake them fresh?" Melissa countered back.

"That sounds amazing."

"Mom makes the best dinner rolls," Sam told him with an exaggerated roll of his eyes. "She drizzles them with honey butter, and I always get a tummy ache from eating too many."

"You'll have to stop me from doing that," Jarod told Sam, as they headed out to his yard. "Let's take the Jeep." He led them over to a large barn and opened the doors to reveal a forest green Jeep Liberty inside. "This is Steve. Hop in."

"You name your vehicles?" Melissa asked on a chuckle.

"Sure. Don't you?" he parried back.

Melissa blushed and then ducked her head, mumbling her answer. "Rella." She glanced at him from beneath her lashes when he turned to Sam for clarification.

"Did she say Rella?"

Sam nodded matter-of-factly. "Yeah, like Cinderella. You know, mom's truck is blue like her dress, and she treats it like it's made of glass. Like Cinderella's slippers."

Jarod bit back a laugh and just shook his head at her. "I don't want to hear a word about my name."

Melissa watched him for a moment and then asked, "So Steve is not just a generic name? Now, you have to tell me which Steve your Jeep is named after."

"Rogers."

Melissa's brows disappeared beneath her stocking cap. "Steve Rogers? *Captain America* Steve Rogers?"

Jarod chuckled with a nod. "Let's head into town. Does Sam need his booster seat? The back row has a jump seat with a shoulder harness. He showed Melissa what he was talking about and she agreed it was a perfect built in solution to smaller passengers.

"That is awesome and will be more than fine. Sam, hop in and get buckled up. Let's go see the town I keep hearing so much about."

Chapter 20

Melissa's mind was spinning with a barrage of ideas, spurred by her face-to-face meetings with the town's shopkeepers. She'd immediately realized that her assumptions had been completely wrong and off-base. Christmas Valley was as close to a real life Christmas town, as she'd ever encountered. From the architectural designs of the buildings to the old town street lights and the elegant gazebo in the town's center to the friendliness of everyone she met; Christmas Valley was a marketing specialist's dream.

She'd met the owners of so many businesses, she'd finally dug a piece of paper from her purse and started jotting everything down. A small bakery. A toy shop that specialized in personalized toys and handmade wooden doll house and train accessories. A combination art gallery and photography studio that was set up for pictures while one waited. They had all sorts of costumes and backdrops to choose from, and Jarod had insisted they all three get a picture taken together to commemorate this Christmas holiday.

There was a diner that looked like something out of a fifty's movie, complete with black and white tile on the floor, polished aluminum countertops, red vinyl booths, and a classic jukebox in the corner. The waitresses wore poodle skirts and even roller skates. The open communication window between the restaurant and the kitchen made the atmosphere complete.

City hall was an ornate building with large stone arches and elaborate stone work, reminding her of pictures she'd seen of European cathedrals. A small library sat next to the city building, complete with Santa's sleigh, eight wire-framed reindeer, and a large red sack appearing to be brimming with toys.

"Whoever was in charge of decorating the town did a remarkable job," she commented to Jarod, as they walked down the sidewalk.

"Oh, everyone helps. They designate the weekend before Thanksgiving as the time for everyone to congregate and get the job done. Now, we all understand that if we were to market Christmas Valley as a tourist spot, we would need to move that date forward…"

"Or make the decorations more permanent," Melissa suggested. As an idea began to form, she started to feel a sense of excitement about being a part of what was happening here, but then doubts began to creep in and she reminded herself she didn't even have the job, let alone could she consider herself part of the community even if she did. She and Sam lived in Denver.

"What was that thought?" Jarod asked, stopping her forward motion with a hand on her shoulder.

She looked up at him, puzzled. "What are you talking about?"

"You asked about the decorations and then your eyes lit up and I could almost see your brain working on something that brought a smile to your lips, but then it faded. All of a sudden. What thought caused that?"

Melissa looked at him and then swallowed. "Well…I was thinking about how the town could be Christmas Valley year round, and I got excited about it. I haven't actually been excited about anything like this for a couple of years now. The festival has been more like a nightmare the last three years between fighting the mayor and the wheels of government on everything from funding to permits."

"And thinking about the festival put that frown and sadness on your face?"

"Was I sad?" she asked, wishing Jarod would just let the subject drop.

"You looked very sad, actually."

Melissa nodded and then made a face. "I guess I was sad. I remembered that not only did I not have the job here, but I also don't live here. I would only be an occasional guest."

"And that made you sad?" Jarod queried, watching her carefully.

Melissa reluctantly nodded. "Yes."

Jarod hooked her arm in his, and they started walking again, catching up to Sam who had stopped to watch in the window of the candle shop; another unique store the town had to offer. "I can answer one of those points right now. The job of helping us market Christmas Valley is yours for the taking. It hasn't been offered to anyone else."

"I just don't see how anyone could do this place justice if they didn't actually live here and weren't part of the community. This place is unique in so many ways…"

"So, move here," Jarod suggested.

"Just like that? Sam and I just pack up our belongings and move to the mountains?"

"Why not?" Jarod challenged her.

"Well…for many reasons."

Jarod nodded and then Sam came running up to them, wanting to go with several boys his own age he'd just met. They were headed to the candy maker's shop. "Can I mom? Please?"

"Where is the candy maker's shop?" she asked.

Jarod pointed across the street. "Right there. Based on the number of kids piling into his shop, he must be pulling taffy. He gloves the kids up and lets them all participate."

"Inventive way of getting the hard work done," Melissa chuckled. She turned to Sam and nodded. "Go ahead but mind your

152

manners."

"I will." Sam turned and called to his new friends, "I can go."

"He makes friends easily," Jarod commented.

"Don't all kids?" Melissa wondered aloud.

"Not all kids. Now, how about we keep walking and meet a few more people?"

"Okay. I can't believe how friendly everyone is being. Did you tell them who I was?"

Jarod shook his head, "Not a word. The mayor knows you're here with me and just the people you've met today."

"But they were all nice before you introduced me."

"Yeah, weird, huh?"

"Not weird, just…I've gotten used to Denver. People are nice, but they don't normally talk to strangers."

"You'll get used to it."

"That's what I'm afraid of," she murmured, as they continued walking. She could easily see herself moving here and becoming a part of this vibrant community. Sam already seemed happy here and, while she'd initially loved her job in Denver, she disliked living in such a big city. She barely saw her neighbors and only knew them by their last names, even though many of them had lived there as long as she had.

Melissa had always dreamed of living someplace where she could walk into the local grocery store and catch up on everything going on in the town because everyone knew everyone else. Some people might dread that kind of life, but she had always longed to feel like she truly belonged somewhere. Christmas Valley was that kind of place.

"So, want to grab some hot cocoa and go sit in the gazebo?

It's kind of the place where couples gather."

Melissa ignored his couples comment but nodded. Sitting down for a bit sounded good. She took the cup of cocoa he handed her a few minutes later and then walked beside him to the center of the town. She could still see the candy maker's shop. Lola, the owner of the local beauty shop, promised to bring him to the gazebo when Sam and her son were finished pulling taffy. The boys were the same age, and Melissa could easily see herself becoming best friends with the red-haired beautician.

"Pick a seat," Jarod invited, as they climbed the three steps leading into the large gazebo.

Melissa headed over to a seat at the edge, looking out over the main street. She wanted to be able to see Sam when he left the candy shop. More importantly, she wanted him to be able to see her. She smiled when she saw the large nativity scene set just to their left.

"I can guess where Sam is going to go when he gets here."

"The nativity set?" Jarod guessed with a smile.

"I'm not sure what the attraction is this year. He spent a lot of time visiting the nativity set at the festival."

Jarod merely nodded and sipped his hot chocolate. After a minute, he turned toward her and then reached out, pushing a loose strand of hair behind her ear. "You still up for taking that moonlit stroll through the trees tonight?"

Melissa tried to ignore the way her heartbeat sped up. It seemed that Jarod was always finding some reason to touch her hand or her shoulder, and now her hair. That tingling sensation was back in her spine and her stomach felt like a whole bevy of butterflies had taken flight.

"You're sure your parents won't mind watching Sam?"

"Positive. My mom is excited to meet you."

"Why would that be?"

"I told them all about you," he told her blandly.

"You talked to your parents about me?" Melissa asked, confusion on her face.

"I did. I needed their advice."

"About me? I don't understand. What exactly did you ask them?"

"I wanted their suggestions on how to convince you to give whatever this is between us a chance. They suggested I invite you here for Christmas, but I had already thought of that suggestion."

"Wait. You invited us here for Christmas because your parents told you to?"

"No but hearing them echo what I was already thinking was reassuring. I invited you and Sam here because I couldn't bear the idea of saying goodbye to you when the festival ended. There's something between us, Melissa, and I don't know about you, but I'm too old to play the crazy dating games the younger generation is into now. I know what I want, and I know when I find it."

Melissa digested his words, having no response at the moment. When she continued to think and remained silent, Jarod reached over and took one of her hands in his and then turned her chin so that she would meet his eyes.

"Just to make sure there are no miscommunications right now. I have found what I want, and that's you and Sam. In my life. In my home. In my future."

"How can you be so sure?" Melissa asked as her common sense tried to tell her that what he was saying was impossible. People didn't fall in love that quickly, did they?

"Let me ask you a question. Do you feel anything for me?"

Melissa nodded, as she replied, "But how can I know if my feelings aren't just a temporary thing?"

"Like your first marriage?" Jarod asked softly.

Melissa sighed and then closed her eyes for a moment. "Sandy said that I needed to stop trying to think everything through and just follow my heart, but I did that once. I wouldn't trade Sam for the entire world, but those first few years were really rough."

"You got hurt." Jarod brushed a finger down her cheek. "I'm sorry that happened to you. Your ex is an idiot."

Melissa chuckled. "On that point I won't argue. Honestly, he was so immature, he would have made a horrible husband in the long run and an even worse father. I just wish I had figured that out before I…before I got emotionally invested."

"I think most people who get to be our ages would say the same thing. It's impossible to go through life and not invest our emotions. Part of that is the risk that someone will trample all over them. I would never do that to you. Or Sam."

"I believe you; I do. I'm just…I'm scared."

Jarod leaned down and kissed her briefly and then settled back against the seat, tucking her against his side. "Me too." After a moment, he whispered in her ear, "But that doesn't mean I don't want to see where this goes."

Melissa thought about that for several minutes and then she suggested, "So, tell me all about yourself."

Jarod chuckled low and asked, "Is this your way of telling me you're willing to try while you're up here?"

Melissa shrugged one shoulder. "Well, I can't very well decide if you're the man I want in my life if all I know about you is that you grow Christmas trees, live in the most awesome place on earth, and can cook."

Before he could respond, Sam came running up to them, excitement in his eyes and his breath coming very fast. "Mom! Mom! Mitch and Deke are here, and they invited me to play catch with them. Can I? Please?"

"Where are they?" Melissa looked past Sam, giving the two high school boys a small wave when she found them. "I see them. Can you stay where I can see you?"

"Sure. So, I can go?"

"I don't see why not. No playing in the street, though."

Sam gave her an exasperated look and a shake of his head. "Mom, I'm not six. I know I shouldn't play around cars."

"I guess I forgot how grown up you're becoming. Go, have fun."

"Well, that seems like providence just shined upon us."

Melissa chuckled and then nodded. "Yes, she did. So, back to my last statement before we were interrupted. Tell me all about yourself."

For the next hour, Jarod and she exchanged stories about their lives. They talked about everything from their favorite color, musical likes and dislikes, books they had read, and they'd even touched on politics. Melissa was amazed that, on every new topic, Jarod seemed to be reading her mind. They complimented one another so well, even those fancy internet dating sites would have been hard pressed to find two people more compatible.

They ate lunch at the diner. Melissa met so many people, she didn't think she'd ever remember their names, but Jarod didn't seemed worried at all. It was a fun meal. Rather than everyone keeping to their own conversation, the diner was like one big happy family meal where people from different tables were talking amongst themselves, loud enough that everyone could hear and participate. It was a meal that Melissa knew she would never forget. She also hoped it wouldn't be the last such meal she shared with Sam and Jarod.

***

"Ready to head back to the cabin, Sam?" Jarod asked as they left the diner.

Sam shook his head, "There's something I need to do first."

Melissa looked confused, "What is it that you need? There's a bathroom in the diner…"

"No, mom. It's nothing like that. Can I go see the nativity set before we leave?"

Melissa shared a look with Jarod, and they both nodded. "Go ahead," she told him. "Want us to go with you?"

"No, I can do this on my own. I promise I won't be long."

"Okay," Melissa smiled and Sam took off.

He'd wanted to go see the nativity when he'd come back from the candy shop, but then Mitch and Deke had surprised him. Sam had been so overjoyed to see them; he hadn't even realized how he'd risen in his own peers' esteem because the older boys wanted to play catch with him. Seeing them had made Sam's day so much brighter, and he couldn't wait to get his mom alone so that he could tell her he never wanted to leave this place.

After a while, Jarod had suggested they go get burgers and milkshakes from the diner, and Sam's stomach had won out. Mitch and Deke had bumped fists with him, promising to catch him again soon. Now that his stomach was full, he was a young man on a mission.

He looked both ways before he crossed the street, not that his mom had anything to worry about in this small town. There was almost no traffic here.

He reached the nativity set and carefully wedged his way between the figurines until he was kneeling next to the manger. This replica of Baby Jesus wasn't nearly as authentic looking as the one in the festival, but Sam reasoned God didn't really mind.

"Baby Jesus, it's me. Sam. So, mom and I are in this really cool town called Christmas Valley up in the mountains. And we're with the neatest guy around. Jarod. I really like him, and he seems to like me. I really wish he could be my dad. He doesn't mind teaching me stuff and he listens when I talk and wants to do silly things...I know that's probably asking a lot. But if it helps, mom seems to like him. I mean, they didn't think I saw them, but they kissed. That means they like each other a lot, right?

"I don't think friends kiss, but then again, I'm only eight. What do I know?

"Anyway, what I wanted to ask was if you could give me one more favor...could we stay here? Mom and I? Please? I made a couple of new friends, and I know mom hasn't really been happy in the city. She's laughing and smiling today, and I really want to see her happy and not so stressed out.

"Guess I'm probably asking for a lot, but if you can figure out a way to let us stay here, I would be really grateful. I don't need anything else for Christmas, just for mom to be happy.

"Gotta go. Thanks for listening."

Sam rushed off to join his mom and Jarod, leaving Joy behind at the nativity. Sam's request was nothing she hadn't heard before, but now it was crunch time and she hoped that Melissa would have enough courage to take a leap of faith. Without it, the plan to bring Sam and his mother happiness was likely fail.

Joy followed the trio back to the cabin, her mind working furiously as she tried to come up with a legal way of helping Melissa find her courage. She'd broken the guardian angel code last year and was determined not to repeat that this year. She'd promised Matthias that she wasn't breaking any rules, and she hadn't. Yet.

Since she wasn't able to influence human emotions, she'd have to rely on Melissa's history to provide the needed push. If only she could find something that would push her that last bit into taking a chance on love.

Chapter 21

After lunch, they headed to the grocery store and then back to Jarod's house to stow everything away and get ready for his family's arrival. Melissa insisted on helping him finish decorating the porch. They had just connected the last string of lights when a dark SUV pulled up and parked.

"That'll be mom and dad. Come one, I'll introduce you."

Melissa hung back while Jarod greeted his mom and then his dad. They hugged and then his mother came straight to her side. "I'm Meredith. You must be Melissa?"

"I am." Melissa extended her hand, but Meredith simply pushed it aside and enveloped her in a big hug. "Handshakes are for strangers and business acquaintances."

Jarod's father was there to take his wife's place when she released Melissa. She was enveloped in the arms of a human teddy bear. "Call me Charlie. Oh, we're so pleased you and your son decided to join us for Christmas. Speaking of which, where is…Sam, is it?"

"He's making snowflakes inside."

"Ah! My favorite past time during the holidays," Meredith smiled. "Charlie, let's go introduce ourselves."

Melissa watched as they walked up the porch and into the cabin, leaving her and Jarod staring after them. She turned to him and asked, "Are they always so…friendly?"

"This is like a second home to them, so yes. Want to help me get their bags?"

"Sure. Are your sisters that friendly?"

"For the most part. They'll be tired of wrangling kids by the time they get here. With any luck the kids will all be ready to sleep, otherwise, we could be in for a long night."

"Tell me again their names," Melissa asked, hoping she could remember a few of the names by the time everyone arrived.

"Laci is married to Jeff and they have three little girls. Arianna, Bekah, and Chloe."

Melissa raised a brow and questioned, "Are they planning to have more children?"

"What you meant to ask was whether or not they intended to name their children after the alphabet. And yes, they did."

"Oh. I was trying to be nice and not offensive."

Jarod chuckled. "You weren't. Jeff is from a family of twelve children so three doesn't seem like many."

"Twelve children? I can't even imagine taking care of that many kids. I can't imagine being pregnant that many times, either."

"You didn't like being pregnant?"

"I didn't like the transition from being pregnant to being a mom. It's kind of a long story, but I wasn't supposed to have Sam for a couple of weeks, so I went to some yard sales with a co-worker in a little town about twenty minutes from home. I went into labor and ended up delivering Sam in the back of the ambulance. Not something I would ever want to do again."

"So, you're not against having more kids?"

"No. I always hoped Sam would have some brothers and sisters, but…"

"…that would mean you'd have to start dating and get married again," Jarod finished for her.

"Yeah. What about you? You've never thought about getting married before?"

"I've thought about it plenty. I've just never met anyone I could see myself spending the next week with, let alone the rest of my life. Until you. You're the first person who's ever checked all the boxes for me."

"I didn't realize I was a checklist," Melissa teased him, understanding what he was saying. Until meeting Jarod, Melissa had given almost no energy to thinking about romance, dating, or a life where she wasn't alone. Jarod was the first man she'd met who had gotten through her barriers and made her think of a different future for herself and her son.

"You're much more than a checklist. That's not what I meant."

"I know what you meant. Can we get back to you telling me about your sisters?"

"How about we finish taking in the luggage and then I'll tell you all about my sisters and their kids? I'll even get out the photo album."

"That would be very helpful," Melissa smiled.

"Here, you take this one, and I'll bring the rest."

They carried the luggage into the cabin and were just in time to witness Meredith and Charlie tossing paper airplanes down the hallway. Sam clapped and then took aim with his own creation.

"Mine went further," Sam jumped up and down excitedly.

"Congratulations Sam," Charlie gave her son a high five.

"What's going on in here? I thought you were making snowflakes to put on the windows?"

"We were, but then Merry suggested we make paper airplanes…"

"…and the rest, as they say, is history," Jarod murmured in

her ear, as he headed down the hallway.

"Well, I think we should tape them in the windows, what do you think?"

"Yay! Jarod will you help us?"

"Of course. My windows have never had paper snowflakes in them before. I can't wait to see what you created."

Twenty minutes later they all stood outside and examined their handiwork. Jarod laid a hand on Sam's shoulder and pronounced, "The cabin has never looked more festive. Thank you, Sam."

Sam nodded and then tugged on her hand. "Mom, can I have a snack."

Melissa smiled and nodded. "Just a little bit of ice cream. You don't want to ruin your dinner."

"Speaking of which, I should probably go make sure the steaks are thawing out correctly. Melissa, do you want to help me?" Jarod nodded toward the kitchen.

"Sure." She followed him into the cabin, relieved that he wasn't going to leave her alone to deal with his parents. She'd seen the speculation in their expressions. It seemed that his mother was looking for an opportunity to get her alone and start her questions. Melissa didn't mind speaking with Jarod's mother, but she wasn't sure she knew the answers herself yet.

She spent the rest of the afternoon working in the kitchen or playing with Sam. Meredith and Charlie settled in the great room by the fireplace, while Jarod busied himself with restocking firewood, and shoveling snow off the sidewalk. His parents seemed focused on Sam. As she watched, her heart hurt because he'd missed having grandparents in his life. It wasn't just a father Sam was missing, he needed family.

Melissa had tried to give Sam everything he needed, within reason, but she didn't have any extended family to give him. She was alone in the world except for Sam and, while she'd adjusted to being alone, it was plain to see that Sam had suffered for the lack of family to love on him. Jarod was lucky. She wasted no time in letting him know that.

True to his word, he retrieved a photo album and showed her pictures of his sisters and their families. In addition to his sister Laci, there was Jennifer and her husband Bryce. They currently only had two children—Shay and Shiloh—but they had made it known that they were trying for a third. At her questioning glance, Jarod had confirmed that Jennifer intended to name all of her children with S names.

"Your sisters seem to like themes."

"A bit. It seems to be the trend these days. Any such trends on your end?"

"No. In fact, I would be more inclined to avoid another name that began with the letter S, just to ensure I wasn't following a trend." Melissa felt a little better about meeting them afterward and was even able to ask appropriate questions during dinner a while later. As the sun began to sink, she started thinking about the walk she was scheduled to take with Jarod. She was surprised to find that she was very nervous.

Spending the day with Jarod, and then the afternoon with his parents, she'd seen what her life could be like if she was to take a chance to see if Jarod's dreams could also be her own. After dinner, she tucked Sam into bed and spent a few extra minutes going over her pros and cons list concerning Jarod.

On the pro list, she had over a dozen things. A job that truly appealed to her. Family and a sense of belonging. Jarod. Great pay. Small town where she might make some real friends. Jarod.

Mountains and an environment that Sam already seemed to be thriving in. Sam would have more family than he could handle. Jarod.

She paused for a moment, realizing she'd added Jarod's name to her list multiple times. "Guess he's more important than I'm wanting to believe," she murmured to herself.

She switched her focus to the con side of the paper. She tapped the pen on the table for almost five minutes without writing a single thing. She couldn't really come up with anything that wasn't merely a space filler. The only true item that belonged on the con list was the simple fact that she could possibly get hurt. Jarod had already assured her he had no intention of that happening. She believed and trusted him, so that meant her con list was empty.

"Melissa? Ready for our walk?" Jarod asked in a whisper from the doorway.

"Yes," she whispered back.

She mentally buoyed herself by thinking about the items on her pro list. This wasn't just a walk beneath the stars. This was a walk that could very well determine the direction her future was headed.

Chapter 22

Jarod waited on the porch with his hands tucked into the pockets of his jacket. Melissa was supposed to meet him out here five minutes ago. The fact that she hadn't arrived made Jarod wonder if she was getting cold feet. He'd been very upfront about his intentions where she and Sam were concerned. She'd also been honest, telling him she was scared of where this thing between them might be heading. No one ever willingly went into a relationship with the intent of getting hurt. He got that.

He heard the front door open and turned to see Melissa step outside. She was pulling on her gloves.

"Sam asleep?" He asked, smiling at her.

"Yes. Have you been waiting out here long?"

"Not really. I thought we would take the ATV out to the trees and then we can walk for a while."

"Okay. It's pretty cold out here."

"I've got blankets you can wrap around your legs."

He helped her get situated in the vehicle and then he slipped behind the steering wheel. He started it up and then turned to look at her. She seemed very nervous. He couldn't have that.

He held out his hand, glove removed, and waited while she removed her own glove and laid her palm across his own. "This is supposed to be fun."

Melissa nodded and forced a smile. "I'm having fun."

"Really? Maybe you should try a real smile then."

Melissa let out a breath and then gave him a more authentic smile. "Guess I'm just nervous. This isn't something I normally do."

"What, look at the stars?" He squeezed her hand and then tucked it beneath the blanket and replaced his glove. "Relax." He moved them toward the trees, keeping the speed down so the wind in their faces wasn't too cold to bear.

"Your parents are very nice. I can't believe how well they and Sam got along. He even wanted them to tuck him in tonight, but I told him he needed to let them rest since they'd travelled most of the day."

"First, they wouldn't have minded at all. Second, I think we've established that my parents are wonderful. My entire family is loving and caring. By the way, my sisters called. They're on their way up here from the airport. From the sound of the kids in the background, my nieces and nephews are wound up. Hopefully, the drive up here will help calm them down, so everyone will be ready to sleep."

"I hope Sam doesn't wake up and wonder where I am." She glanced back toward the way they'd come. She looked worried.

"Will Sam be upset if he does wake up?"

"Honestly, I don't know. I haven't ever done anything like this. Given how quickly he took to your parents, I'm sure he'll be fine."

"Well, in that case, I suggest we enjoy ourselves to the fullest." Jarod parked the ATV and then came around and helped her out. "There's a bench out that direction where we can sit and watch the sky."

"Do you come out here often?"

"Yes. Actually, this is my favorite spot on the entire farm. It overlooks the wilderness area." He took hold of her hand and led her to a hand-carved wooden bench. It was nestled in a small clearing, surrounded by the Christmas trees, some of which had been strung with tiny white lights. As if by magic, the trees came to life, bathing the bench is warm light.

"This is amazing," she told him in a reverent tone.

"Thanks. Have a seat and then I'll kill the lights, so we can see every star possible."

Melissa did so and then Jarod joined her, sitting close enough that their thighs were touching. He opened a box next to the bench and withdrew several heavy blankets. He draped one over both of their laps before killing the small lights.

"Look up," he whispered next to her ear, wrapping an arm around her shoulders so that her head had something to rest against as she looked up. "Let your eyes adjust for a few minutes and tell me when you can see the Milky Way."

Melissa did as he asked. She watched for several long moments before suddenly, in the sky above her, there was a ribbon of star so dense it appeared as a winding wave or cloud of heavenly bodies. The Milky Way. She'd never seen it so prominently displayed.

As she watched the sky, it seemed to come to life before her eyes. A shooting star moved across the sky, and then she watched several things moving across the sky. "Look! What is that?"

Jarod followed her finger and then smiled, "A satellite. If you watch long enough, you'll see several of them over the course of a few hours. I've even been able to see the International Space Station a few times. It's much larger than those other satellites and unmistakable once you've seen it the first time."

"I have to tell you; this is pretty cool. Sam would enjoy learning about the stars."

And there's no way he'll ever have this kind of opportunity living in the big city.

"We'll bring him out here," Jarod offered.

A companionable silence settled over the landscape. They watched the stars. Minute by minute, Melissa seemed to relax more. After a while, he looked at her and whispered, "Sleeping?"

"No," she whispered back. "I was just sitting here trying to remember a time when I felt so at peace. It's kind of ironic if you think about it. It's almost Christmas, and I've been displaced from my home. I'm losing my job in a few weeks. Yet...I'm not worried. I should be worried, shouldn't I?"

Jarod reached over and brushed his thumb across her cheek. "What good would worrying do for you?"

"Absolutely nothing," she immediately replied. "I know that. But, it's my go-to thing when life gets hard."

"I think we all do that sometimes. What did you think of the town, now that you've had some time to process everything you saw this morning?"

"Christmas Valley is..." She paused and then turned her head to meet his eyes. "It's magical. You all have a wonderful idea of turning this into a little slice of the North Pole."

"You have some ideas for how to market it?"

"I have a ton of ideas. Not just for how to market it during the holiday season but year round."

"So, you've decided to take the job offer?"

Melissa sighed and then settled back against his arm again. "I don't know. I've always been so careful when making decisions. I make lists of pros and cons and weigh the long-term benefits of my decision, not only for myself but also for Sam."

"Have you done that yet?"

"I have," she nodded. "But that's my problems. I could only come up with one thing to put on the con list."

"Only one? What was it? Maybe I can help?"

Melissa sat up and then turned and looked at him. "The only thing on my con list was getting hurt."

"By me?" Jarod questioned, also sitting up and facing her.

"No. I know you would never intentionally hurt me or Sam. I just…what if we're moving too fast?"

Jarod was quiet for a long moment before he leaned forward, his lips just a breath from hers, and whispered, "There will always be 'what ifs'. How about you listen to your heart and not your head?"

"Is that what you're doing?"

"Yes," he whispered, closing the distance between their lips and kissing her with all the feelings he was holding inside. He closed his eyes when she did the same, savoring the feel of her in his arms.

When they were both breathless, he lifted his head and placed tender kisses across her cheek, nuzzling behind her ear for a moment before whispering, "What's your heart telling you now?"

Melissa tipped her head back, giving him better access to her throat and murmured, "That I would be crazy not to go for it."

Jarod moved back and then asked, "Does that mean you're willing to give us a chance? Or, are you going to take the job?"

"Yes. And, yes."

Jarod pulled her into his arms and started placing kisses across her face, ending up at her lips once again. "This is the best night."

Melissa giggled and nodded. "I agree."

They sat there for a long time after that, watching the stars and talking about the future. By the time Jarod drove her back to the cabin, his sisters and their families had arrived, and everyone had gone to bed. Jarod couldn't be sad about that turn of events, liking the fact that he could walk Melissa to her room and kiss her goodnight without an audience or having to answer all sorts of questions. Knowing his sisters, there would be plenty of time for that later.

Chapter 23

Christmas Eve in Heaven…

"Hallelujah! Let Heaven and Earth Rejoice! Christ the newborn King is born in Bethlehem! Glory in the Highest! Peace on the Earth!"

The angel choir finished the song with their wings and arms uplifted, their voices raised as they proclaimed the arrival of Christmas. A glow from the palace in the center of Heaven had them all beaming at a job well done as God and His Son showed their approval.

Joy bid her friends goodbye and started to head back down to witness Sam and his mother's evening, but Matthias stopped her.

"Just a minute, Joy. A word, please?"

Joy swallowed and then hesitantly approached the larger angel. "Yes? Did you need something?"

"You seem awfully joyful tonight. How are things with your young charge?"

Joy smiled. "They're going very well. His mother decided to accept the job in Christmas Valley and give a relationship with the Christmas tree man a try."

Matthias frowned. "Didn't they just meet a week or so ago?"

"Yes, but who's to say how long true love takes?" she countered back.

"True love indeed." Matthias placed his hands on his hips and scowled at her. "Okay, how many angel codes did you break?"

"None. Angel promise. I didn't have to do anything. Melissa's own conscience and her inner desires took care of

173

everything."

"You didn't play on her emotions?"

"I didn't have to. I have to tell you I thought about it, but only for a moment. I was going to try and find something in her past to help create the emotion needed, but she did that all on her own."

"If I find out differently, there will be consequences," Matthias warned her.

Joy beamed another smile at him. "You don't have anything to worry about. Everything is going to work out just fine. Better than fine. Fabulous."

Matthias shook his head and then waved his hand at her. "Be off with you. Go spread your angel joy elsewhere."

"Yes, sir." Joy headed back down to earth, relieved that she'd not had to break any rules this time around. It was truly turning out to be one of the best Christmases ever, well…except for the very first Christmas. Nothing could ever come close to being better than that.

***

Christmas Eve in Jarod's Cabin…

"Alright kids, it's time to gather around for the reading of the Christmas story," Meredith called out, her voice permeating the entire cabin. People came from all over, gathering around the chairs and couches while some sat on the floor and others settled onto the rug in front of the fire.

When everyone was assembled, Meredith nodded at her husband, who produced a large family Bible. Melissa was sitting on the floor with Sam leaning up against her legs. She started to shift her position, only to find Jarod slipping behind her and providing a place for her to lean back. She glanced around nervously, wondering how everyone else was taking his blatant show of affection. His sisters were sitting in almost the same position with their husbands and children. No one was paying her and Jarod any attention.

"Twas the night before Christmas, and all through the house. Not a creature was stirring. Not even a mouse."

"Grandpa, that's not the real Christmas story. Did you forget again?" Arianna spoke up.

Charlie scratched his head and then nodded. "I'm sorry, darlin'. I guess I did. Why don't you and the other children tell the story this year?"

"Yay! We know this," Shiloh agreed.

"I'll start." Nine-year old Arianna stood up. She waited until everyone was quiet and then she began to speak. "So, Joseph and Mary lived in Nazareth, and the ruler of the land told everyone they had to go to their hometown to register and pay their taxes. Mary was pregnant at the time, but they made the journey back to Bethlehem. When they got there, it was night and they couldn't find any place to stay. Mary was getting ready to have her baby. Joseph found an innkeeper who said they could use his barn, so that's where Joseph took Mary, and that's where she delivered the baby. They chose the name Jesus."

Shiloh stood up, "My turn. There were shepherds on the hillside outside Bethlehem watching their sheep. Suddenly, there was a great host of angels in the sky. They told the frightened shepherds to go see the newborn King and that a star would show them the way."

"What does a host of angels sound like?" Four-year-old Chloe asked.

"Like thunder," Sam offered. "At least, that's what my Sunday school teacher, Mrs. Barnes, told us."

"I like that explanation," Jarod told him with a smile.

"You forgot the wise men," Shay complained. At five-years-old, Shay was very particular about how things were done. Leaving the wise men out was a grave error.

"Okay," Bekah piped up. She had just turned seven and was the tomboy of the three girls. She and Sam had found many things to do the last two days—not all of them parent approved—but it was Christmas, so the mud on the floor had been forgotten when everyone saw the snow family the duo had created out behind the cabin.

"The wise men studied the stars and, when the new star appeared, they packed up their camels and started following it. When King Herod heard what they were doing, he invited them to his palace and said he wanted them to find the baby and then come back and tell him, so he could go see him as well."

"King Herod was lying. He only wanted to kill the Baby Jesus," Sam added.

"That's right," Meredith nodded. "King Herod was so upset when the wise men didn't come back that he ordered all of the babies under the age of two years old to be killed."

"Why two years?" Arianna asked. "I forgot."

"Well, the wise men had to travel a long way. It took them almost two years before they reached King Herod. When they found the baby, he wasn't a tiny infant any longer, but a toddler."

"That's right. They brought gifts to the baby. Joseph used the gifts to help them all escape to Egypt."

"That's right," Charlie smiled at his grandchildren. "It seems you children have been paying attention. How about I finish up the story?"

"Yay!" the children clapped and cheered him on.

"God sent Baby Jesus to the world because it was the only way we could ever gain forgiveness for our sins. Jesus came to the earth so that he could grow up and perform miracles, so people could come to know who God was. He was born, so he could later die and then rise again and defeat the powers of Hell."

Charlie paused and then leaned forward and whispered, "But that's a story for Easter time. Tonight, we're celebrating the birth of Jesus. Now, how about we do that by opening one present each?"

The children all started talking at once, even Sam joined in. Melissa was very glad that she'd done all of her Christmas shopping for him online and that everything had arrived prior to them leaving Denver.

Jarod had been wonderful about finding hiding places for them. Last night, he'd even stayed up late and helped her wrap them. His sisters and their husbands had done the same thing. The six adults had eaten popcorn and exchanged horror stories about Christmas presents gone awry; like when the gifts needed to be put together because nothing ever worked correctly.

Thankfully, Melissa hadn't gotten Sam anything that required the use of tools or wood glue this year. Jarod had been surprisingly adept at gift wrapping and making bows. She'd finally turned over all of the bow making to him.

"Which gift can I open, mom?" Sam bounced up and down in front of her.

"Let me," Jarod offered, standing up and retrieving one of the gifts he'd purchased for Sam. Sam's eyes lit up when he saw how big the box was, and he immediately started tearing the paper off.

Jarod sat back down, pulling Melissa back against his chest and murmuring in her ear, "Shay and Shiloh are opening *Nerf* guns as well. Something tells me chaos is going to ensue for the remainder of my sisters' visit."

"You could always tell them they can't fire them in the house. Maybe they could use the barn?" Melissa offered.

"That's the perfect compromise. Tomorrow. Not tonight. Guess we'll have to deal with a little chaos before bedtime. What's the fun in opening a gift you're forbidden to use?"

Melissa smiled, adding yet another mark in the positive column where Jarod was concerned. The three boys had their guns open now and, after removing the packaging and figuring out how to load them with the foam darts, it became a war against the girls who had all opened up dress-up kits, complete with makeup and plastic shoes.

Meredith and Charlie took sides and soon an all-out war was taking place in the cabin. The boys were hiding behind furniture, and the girls were sneaking up on them and trying to put makeup on their cousins. Through it all, Sam held his own. Melissa had to hold back tears of happiness and regret for not having seen that he needed this before now.

"What's that look for?" Jarod asked.

"I was just watching Sam and seeing how much he's needed this. I guess I should have…"

"Don't do that," Jarod advised her. "You've done a wonderful job with Sam. Don't start second guessing yourself. You'll just make yourself upset for nothing. The past can't be changed."

"I know," she sighed.

"Let's go make some hot cocoa and hopefully that will calm everyone down, so we can get to bed sometime before midnight. This crew wakes up early on Christmas morning."

Chapter 24

Christmas Morning…

"Mom," Sam's voice came through the closed bedroom door. When Melissa didn't immediately answer, Sam used their secret code of knocks and then called her name again. "Mom! It's Christmas! You have to get up."

"I'm coming," she called out, swinging her legs over the side of the bed. She yawned and then stretched her arms up over her head, rolling her head to work out a few kinks.

Melissa hadn't gotten more than a few hours of sleep the night before. She'd been up thinking about everything Jarod had said to her, his kisses, and the way he and his family were interacting with Sam. The final blow had come when Sam had insisted on having Jarod tuck him into bed.

Melissa had agreed and then stood idly by while Jarod read him a bedtime story. Jarod had even used voices for the various characters in the story. Sam had been enthralled. When Jarod had closed the book and started to rise, her son had thrown himself into Jarod's arms and hugged him fiercely. His whispered, "I love you, Jarod," had almost undone her.

Melissa had seen the shock and then acceptance on Jarod's face. She'd felt tears sting her eyes when Jarod had whispered back to him, "I love you two, buddy. Sleep tight."

Melissa's emotions had been erratic, but she'd pretended not to have heard their exchange. Jarod had escorted her back to the bedroom she was using, stopping her just outside the door.

"Anything wrong?" he'd asked her.

Melissa had opened her mouth to explain how she was feeling, but at the last minute, she'd changed her mind. "I think I'm just tired."

"Baking four dozen cookies will do that to a person."

Melissa gave him a half smile. "How do you know?"

"Just because I don't have kids of my own doesn't mean I've escaped having nieces and nephews without acquiring an appreciation for the local bakery. In my case, it wasn't just any cookies, it was frosted Christmas cookies."

Jarod gave a little shiver of revulsion at the memory. "I have an aversion to decorated sugar cookies to this day. But, on a more serious note, I had a really great day."

"Me too." He'd kissed her and then asked her if she would consider taking an even greater leap of faith. With him. By agreeing to marry him when her job in Denver was up.

The question had taken her completely by surprise. She'd escaped into the sanctuary of her bedroom before he could say another word. She'd then lain awake most of the night, trying to decide if he was serious or not.

Melissa had known that marriage was where Jarod hoped they would end up. She didn't have any objections to the matrimonial state, especially when it came to Jarod. It was just happening so fast! They'd only known one another for two weeks. Two weeks!

Was it even possible to fall in love in two weeks? It happens that way, sometimes even faster, in the movies, but in real life? How was one to know if the other person is the one they're destined to spend the rest of their mortal life with? In fact, how is one to know that they're really in love and what they're feeling isn't just a passing phase?

Noises from beyond the closed bedroom door reminded her that she was expected momentarily to make an appearance in her pajamas, as was the custom in Jarod's family. She'd seen the look of pleasure on Sam's face when Arianna had explained their family's custom of opening their presents on Christmas morning in their pajamas, taking a family photo afterwards, and then eating breakfast before getting dressed for the day. Being included was something even her eight year old had been able to comprehend. Inclusion. Sam seemed to thrive on it.

"Mom? Aren't you coming? Everyone else is waiting."

Melissa's eyes closed for a moment and then she scrambled from the bed, assuring him, "I'm coming. Give me another minute to brush my teeth."

She hurried to the attached bathroom to quickly prepare. She hoped her restless night wouldn't be visible to anyone. She grabbed her robe and wrapped it around her t-shirt and pajama pants, feeling very self-conscious as she opened the door and peeked out.

"Good morning," a voice to her right startled her. She'd been trying to see those gathered around the Christmas tree in the great room and hadn't seen Jarod standing in the hallway waiting for her.

"Merry Christmas," she murmured to him.

Jarod smiled and then approached her, daring her with his eyes to stand her ground and not retreat into the bedroom. "Merry Christmas, Melissa." He lowered his head and kissed her, making her glad she'd taken the extra minute to brush her teeth.

He'd done the same, tasting of mint toothpaste and the unique flavor she'd come to associate with him. He smelled wonderful. She inhaled his aftershave, noticing by the smoothness of his jaw that he'd also taken the time to shave this morning. She closed her eyes in appreciation and kept them closed long after he withdrew from their kiss.

When she could feel him watching her, she opened her eyes and became trapped by his gaze.

"You didn't sleep last night," he stated. He searched her eyes and then added, "Neither did I."

"Are you guys coming?" Sam called from the end of the hallway.

"Give us a minute, Sam. We'll be right there," Jarod answered, his eyes never leaving Melissa's face.

"He's going to keep bothering us," she whispered.

"I know. I've already heard from most of my nieces and nephews along with Sam. They're anxious to open their gifts. They'll have to wait for a minute. Come with me." Jarod pulled her hand and led her down the hallway to the backdoor of the cabin. It led to a small porch that overlooked the farm and the wilderness beyond.

"Brrr," she told him as he pulled her outside.

"I'm sorry, but unfortunately, this is the only place beside the hallway closet I could think of where we might have a moment to ourselves."

"The hallway closet?" she asked with a frown.

"My nieces are convinced it's full of spiders and refuse to go near it. My nephews planted that idea in their head yesterday morning while they were plotting how to get even with the girls for winning the snowball fight earlier that morning."

"And Sam," Melissa asked, not sure where he'd fit into this scenario.

"He was the reason the girls won the snowball fight."

"Ah, that explains why he spent the rest of the day playing with the girls and not your nephews. They think he was a traitor. They don't realize that Sam's ignorant of the way these things work and where his allegiance should lie. He likes to champion the underdogs."

"It's okay. I explained it to him and to them. Everyone is fine now."

Melissa was starting to shiver, and she turned back toward the door. "Let's go back inside."

"Wait. Not yet. I wanted to ask you something, and I didn't want you to feel any pressure to answer a certain way. I wouldn't put you in that kind of position."

Melissa watched as Jarod pulled a small black box from the pocket of his flannel robe. "Melissa, I know we've only known one another a few weeks, but I know my heart. It's belonged to you since the first time I saw you. I didn't realize what I was feeling at that time but having you and Sam here these last few days has helped me clarify the situation."

He studied her face briefly before saying, "I love you. Not as a friend, although I hope we will always be one another's best friends. I don't love you like my sisters, although I will tell you they have both confided in me that they love you and, if I don't make you part of our family, they are going to disown me."

Melissa's mouth fell open in shock. "They didn't."

Jarod nodded. "They did, and my parents sided with them when I dared to complain. They didn't have to threaten me because I've known what I wanted for almost a week now. I want you and Sam in my life. I want to be there when Sam goes on his first date or learns to drive a truck. I want to watch him graduate high school, and I want to be there when he falls in love the first time and has a million questions he needs to voice."

Jarod was verbalizing everything she'd dreamed about when she had fallen asleep early this morning. She felt tears spill over her cheeks, but, before she could wipe them away herself, Jarod was there, using his thumbs to dry her cheeks.

"Are those happy tears?"

Melissa nodded. "Yes. I have spent so many years alone, focused on raising Sam, that I didn't realize I'd locked away my heart where people other than him were concerned. I'm tired of being alone. Of crying into my pillow after he goes to bed because I need to talk to someone, and there's no one there."

When Jarod opened his mouth to speak, she laid a gentle finger over his lips. "Let me finish, please?"

He nodded, so she continued, "When we first came here and you started talking about the future, I wanted it so badly that I automatically started telling myself it was never going to happen so that I wouldn't be disappointed when my dire prediction came true. And then I saw how you were with Sam. I saw how you interacted with the townspeople. I met your family and realized that you are a product of your environment; one I have only dreamed of ever belonging to."

She paused for a moment and then stepped forward and cupped his cheek. "Jarod, I always thought love at first sight was a myth made up to sell books and movies. You proved to me that it really does happen. It's happened to me. I know I speak for my son when I tell you we both love you."

Jarod's eyes flooded with relief, as he gathered her close and hugged her while kissing her until they were both breathless. "Thank God. I thought you were getting ready to tell me you'd decided against the job and me."

"If I left here now, I'd be leaving a large chunk of my heart; a chunk I don't think I would ever be able to replace or fill."

"Then stay here with me. Take the job with the town and marry me. Become my wife and help me build a legacy to leave behind for our children..."

"Children?" she asked, breathlessly and with a waver in her voice as she shivered in the cold.

"We need to go inside, but first I need to ask my question." Jarod slipped to one knee and held the box out. "Melissa, will you honor me by becoming my wife? Will you share your son with me and build a future here in Christmas Valley with me?"

Melissa swallowed and then nodded, "I will. Crazy at this all seems, I think it would break my heart to say no. So, yes. Yes, I will marry you."

Cheers and applause broke out from behind the closed door. She blushed, knowing everyone inside had been eavesdropping. Jarod slipped the ring onto her finger and then stood up and kissed her passionately, gaining them both catcalls and whistles from everyone who was now watching through the opened doorway.

She shivered again and Jarod chuckled. "Time to get you inside before you become a frozen bride."

She nodded and then blushed when she saw everyone was still watching them. "Don't they have presents to open?"

"Most definitely. Off with the lot of you. Go open your presents, or I'm going to have Santa come and take them all away."

The adults grinned knowingly, but little Shay was truly concerned and asked, "Can Uncle Jarod do that? I don't want Santa to take my presents away."

"I think Uncle Jarod is just teasing. Let's go open the presents and see what Santa brought you," his father Bryce told him.

"That was mean," Melissa told him.

"I'll apologize later. So, now that you've agreed to marry me. Want to tie the knot on New Year's Eve?"

"That's not even a week away," she told him, as he led her inside and then closed the outside door.

"So? Think about it. We could start the New Year off as a couple."

"I have to go back to Denver. Did you forget that?"

"Not at all. There's not much for me to do during this time of year here at the farm. I can go with you until your time working for the city is up, and we can come up here on the weekends when Sam is out of school."

"This all seems like it's happening so fast."

"Then marry me, and we'll figure out the rest. What do you say?"

They'd reached the end of the hall and she could see that everyone was watching for them to join in the festivities. She could see the happiness on Meredith and Charlie's faces. As for Sam, he was excitedly telling Shay and Shiloh that he now had a dad, too. Their uncle was going to be his new dad, so that made him their cousins as well as the girls. He said it with so much pride and happiness, she felt her heart overflow with joy.

She turned around and wrapped her arms around Jarod's neck. "New Year's Day sounds like a better plan."

"New Year's Day it is." They kissed before he called out to their audience, "Let's get these presents opened. We have a wedding to plan."

Epilogue

Guardian Angel School…

Joy was so pleased with how things were working out for Sam. She combed the school rooms until she finally found Matthias sitting with Theo and several other angels. He turned when he sensed her presence, his forehead frowning for a moment and then smoothing out as he realized she was brimming with happiness.

"Excuse me," he told the other angels. He came to her and asked, "Do I need to clean up any messes?"

Joy shook her head. "No. I did it. Sam's dream and request is coming true, but I didn't have to break any rules to make it happen."

"Not a one?" Matthias asked.

"Not a one. True love won this time. Sam got everything he asked for and then some. His mom is no longer lonely, and Sam gained a dad."

"So, everything worked out well."

"Better than well. Almost like magic."

"Well, tis the Season," Matthias told her with a cheesy grin.

Joy couldn't take issue with the statement and did a little twirl before settling down once more. "The Season of Miracles."

"I'm happy for you and for your young charge. Do you want to continue to oversee Sam, or would you like a new challenge?"

"Oh, I want to stay with Sam. There's so much in store for him, and I want to be there by his side to help him navigate life on earth."

"Very well. So, it shall be," Matthias told her.

Joy hugged him spontaneously, getting chuckles from the

187

other angels. "Sorry."

"Don't be. Was there anything else?"

"Have you seen Hope or Charity today?"

"No, I haven't. I believe they are still with their charges."

"Oh. Well, I guess I'll see them soon. I'm going to go watch Sam celebrate. Merry Christmas, Matthias."

"Merry Christmas, Joy. Now and every day of the year."

Joy smiled and then joined Sam and his newly acquired family as they exchanged gifts and ate way too much food. It was a normal human celebration but, for Sam and his mother, they'd been given a gift this year that would change the course of their lives. Love. The greatest miracle of all.

Sample Story

Christmas Angel Hope, Three Christmas Angels Book Two

Thank You

Dear Reader,

Thank you for choosing to read my books out of the thousands that merit reading. I recognize that reading takes time and quietness, so I am grateful that you have designed your lives to allow for this enriching endeavor, whatever the book's title and subject.

Now more than ever before, Amazon reviews and Social Media play vital role in helping individuals make their reading choices. If any of my books have moved you, inspired you, or educated you, please share your reactions with others by posting an Amazon review as well as via email, Facebook, Twitter, Goodreads, -- or even old-fashioned face-to-face conversation! And when you receive my announcement of my new book, please pass it along. Thank you.

For updates about New Releases, as well as exclusive promotions, visit my website and sign up for the VIP mailing list. Click here to get started: www.morrisfenrisbooks.com

I invite you to visit my Facebook page often
facebook.com/AuthorMorrisFenris where I post not only my news,
but announcements of other authors' work.

For my portfolio of books on Amazon, please visit my Author Page:

Amazon USA:
amazon.com/author/morrisfenris

Amazon UK:
https://www.amazon.co.uk/Morris%20Fenris/e/B00FXLWKRC

You can also contact me by email:
authormorrisfenris@gmail.com

With profound gratitude, and with hope for your continued reading
pleasure,

Morris Fenris
Author & Publisher

Made in the USA
Monee, IL
28 November 2020

49838301R00111